THE GUNSMITH

464

The Ticket Clerk

THE GUNSMITH

464

The Ticket Clerk

J.R. Roberts

SPEAKING VOLUMES, LLC
NAPLES, FLORIDA
2020

The Ticket Clerk

ISBN 978-1-64540-347-0

Chapter One

The plan was perfect—at least, it had been so far. Three stagecoach robberies and three very good hauls.

Carl Walker looked up as the door to his office opened and the woman entered. She was wearing a high-necked dress that extended past her knees and a hat with half a veil covering her face. As she came closer, he saw that she had to be in her fifties, although she moved with youthful strides.

"Can I help you, Ma'am?"

"Yes, sir," she said. "I need to buy a ticket on your next stage."

"That won't be til tomorrow, Ma'am."

"Oh really?" she said, looking dismayed. "I guess I'll need to get a room for the night."

"The hotel down the street offers discounts for stage-line passengers," he told her.

"Really? Thank you for telling me that, although money isn't a problem."

"And how far will you be going on the stage tomorrow?" he asked.

"As far as it goes."

"That'd be all the way to Denver," he said.

"Fine."

He told her the price of the ticket, and she paid him, from a roll of bills she had in her purse.

He made out her ticket and handed it to her. Across the top was painted THE COLORADO STAGELINE.

"Do you own this line?" she asked, as if she suddenly was in no hurry to leave the office.

"No, Ma'am," he said. "I'm just a ticket clerk."

"I see." She hesitated. "You just seem old enough to be the owner."

He smiled.

"I'm thirty-five, Ma'am," he said, "and I like my job just fine."

"Of course, of course. I didn't mean—thank you for your time." She still hesitated.

"Is there something else I can do for you?" he asked.

"I—I don't know anyone here," she said. "I just came in today—I wonder, would you be willing to have supper with me tonight? I'm—I'm quite alone, and—"

"I'd be real happy to have supper with you, Ma'am," he said. "I'm Carl." He put his hand out.

"Carl," she said shaking his hand. "I'm Amanda."

"Can I come by the hotel to get you at, say, seven?" he asked.

"Seven would be fine," she said. "Yes, that would be just fine. I'll see you then, Carl."

She turned and walked away, moving with a nice sway in her step, as if she knew he was watching her.

***

Later that night, after supper, Carl walked Amanda back to her hotel.

"That was a very pleasant meal, Carl," she said. "Thank you."

The dress she wore to supper was a little fancier than the one she'd been wearing that afternoon, and there was no veil to cover her face. She had obviously been a beauty once but now fading, was still pretty and appeared to have a nice shape beneath the dress.

He invited himself up to her room and she went along with it. As soon as they entered, he grabbed her by the shoulders and roughly pushed her down on the bed.

"Carl!" she said. "What are you—"

"Come on," he said to her, "isn't this what you wanted when you asked me to have supper with you?"

"Well, not exactly—"

"Sure it is," he said. He reached down, grabbed the front of her dress with both hands and yanked it apart. Buttons flew across the room.

"Carl!" She said, but didn't object. Her breathing quickened as he sat her up and yanked the dress down so that her breasts poured out. They were large and pale, with dark nipples. She had a nice body for a woman in her fifties, so he figured he was going to enjoy this.

He stepped back, undid his trousers, yanked them down. His already hard cock sprang free.

"Oh my . . ." she gasped, staring.

He turned, sat on the bed and ordered, "Help me off with my boots."

With her dress down around her waist she got to her knees in front of him and pulled off his boots.

"Now the trousers," he said.

She grabbed his pants and yanked them down to his ankles and then off. After that she ran her hands up and down his bare legs and thighs before taking his cock in one hand and stroking it.

"You young men, you can last a long time, can't you?" she asked.

"As long as you want, Amanda," he said.

He grabbed her, pulled her to him and roughly kissed her, long and hard enough to make her lips swell.

Abruptly, he turned them both and pushed her onto her back on the bed, then grabbed the bottom of her dress and pulled it off, further ripping it. He then tore at her petticoats and pantaloons until he had her completely naked. Now he could see the thickness of her waist and thighs that had come with age, but there was nothing unpleasant about the sight. He grabbed her ankles, pulled her legs apart, and drove his hard cock into her already wet depths . . .

Chapter Two

He fucked her for a long time while she was on her back, then turned her over. He leaned in and pressed his face to hers, his still hard penis rubbing against her ass cheeks.

"This is what you want, isn't it?" he asked. "Not to be alone?"

"Yes, oh yes," she said, her face pressed to the pillow.

"I thought so," he said. "The minute you walked in I knew you wanted this."

He spread her thighs so he could slide between them and up into her vagina, again.

"And this?" he said, driving in and out of her so hard the bed moved.

"Yes!" she cried, "Yes, yes, yes!"

For a moment he considered fucking her in her ass, like he'd done once with a French whore, but he didn't think she was ready for that, yet . . . maybe later. So he continued to take her this way, burying himself as deeply in her as he could. Finally exploding and emptying himself into her . . .

***

"Can't you stay?" she asked, as he dressed. "I—I wanted to take you in my mouth."

"As nice as that sounds," he said, "I can't stay all night. I have some business to take care of."

She got to her knees on the edge of the bed and reached for him.

"Then come back," she said. "When you're finished with your business, come back. She touched her swollen lips. "I want . . . more."

He went to her, then, and kissed her brutally.

"All right," he promised, "I'll be back."

"I'll leave the door unlocked," she said. "If I'm asleep, just . . . wake me any way you want."

"Don't worry," he said. "I will."

***

Colorado Springs had grown from a town almost into a city over the years. The population had swelled to seventeen thousand. Pike's Peak had brought tourists from all over the world, and so many had come from as far as England that there was an area called "Little

London." Many of the Brits had even invested in the Denver and Rio Grande Railroad.

But the Colorado Stageline still had routes extending in every direction, and there were those people who preferred to travel by coach rather than train. Carl didn't know how much longer that would continue, but he was determined to take advantage of it for as long as he could.

He went to the Monument Saloon, named after Monument Creek, at the base of Pike's Peak. It was one of the largest saloons in town, therefore the perfect place to blend in while meeting with undesirables.

There was a back room that was used for private poker games or meetings. As Carl Walker entered, he saw that Damian Mair had already arrived with his partner, Albert Lee. There with beers in front of them and a third beer waiting for him.

"Gotcha one," Damian said, pointing.

"Thanks." Carl sat and drank down half the beer. He needed it after his session with Amanda.

Albert watched, then asked, "Whatayou been doin'?"

"I've been doin' research," Carl said. "Are you gents ready for tomorrow?"

"As long as there's a stage," Damian said, "we're ready."

"There's a stage, and there'll be a lockbox on it. But there's also going to be a woman inside. Make sure you get her purse."

"Why's that?" Albert Lee asked.

"Because she's got a big roll of bills in it," Carl said. "It could choke a horse."

"Are you sure?" Damian asked.

"I saw it when she paid for her ticket."

"Any other passengers?" Al Lee asked.

"A couple, but they won't have anything. It's up to you if you want a watch or a ring from them. Or a bag filled with ladies things."

"Haw!" Damian laughed loudly. "That'd be funny if we took those."

"And remember," Carl said, "don't kill anybody. In fact, don't hurt anybody. Once that happens, there'll be too much law, and we'll have to move on."

"We gotcha, Carl," Damian said. "We rob 'em, we don't hurt 'em."

"An' we don't kill 'em," Albert Lee chimed in.

"Right."

Carl finished his beer and stood up.

"Where you off to?" Damian asked. "Don't ya want another beer?"

"No," Carl said, "fact is, I still got a lot of research to do."

Chapter Three

Carl was pleasantly exhausted the next morning. He'd gone back to Amanda's room, taken her in the ass, her mouth, and a few more positions he could think of, just because she was a lonely woman. In the end, he left her and went back to his own room. He slept soundly but rose early enough to have breakfast and get to work on time.

The passengers sat on a bench near his desk, waiting for the stage to start boarding. Amanda looked very proper in her traveling suit, but every so often would steal a glance over at him. Nobody looking at her would ever believe what he had been doing with her the night before. It was a bonus for him, a pleasant diversion—and truth be told, a bonus for her, as well. Of course, it might not make up for losing her money, but there was no way he was going to pass up that roll of bills she was carrying. If he hadn't given her a night that was worth the money, he'd certainly given her one that she'd remember.

The door opened and the driver, Highway Bill Dolan, stuck his head in and nodded at Carl.

"Okay, folks," Carl called out, "time to board."

Amanda stood and walked to the stage with none of the sway that had been in her step the day before. But the other two passengers—both men—followed behind and ogled her, anyway.

Now all Carl Walker had to do was sit and wait.

***

"Ma'am," Highway Bill said to Amanda, "can I help you in?" He extended his hand.

"Thank you," Amanda said, accepting the assistance.

"Here ya go," the drummer said, handing Bill his case containing hair samples. He climbed into the back of the stage after Amanda.

"Catch!" Highway Bill yelled and tossed the case up to Shotgun Sammy Slade.

"Got it!" Sammy said, catching the case and securing it up top.

The other man had no such baggage and simply entered the rear of the stage. The two men sat opposite the woman and admired her.

Shotgun Sammy dropped down from the top of the stage and spit a stream of brown tobacco juice into the dirt.

"Ready to go?" he asked Highway Bill.

"Yeah, we're ready," Bill said, "Let's climb aboard."

The two men climbed atop the stage, and Highway Bill picked up the reins and put his hand on the brake.

"Hopefully," he said, "we don't get robbed today."

Shotgun Sammy spat a stream of tobacco and said, "That's what we're hoping for."

Bill released the break and shook the reins at the team.

***

"Don't forget," Damian Mair said to the three men riding with him. "They've got a shotgun on the stage."

"We'll take care of 'im," one of the men said.

"Hey," Albert lee said, "we got orders not to kill anybody."

"Then how do we take care of the guy ridin' shotgun?" the fourth man asked.

"We'll have to take them without firin' a shot," Damian said.

"You think we can do that?" one of the men asked.

"If we don't," Al Lee said, "we're gonna be out of our jobs."

"You got that?" Damian asked the other two men.

"Yeah, we got it," one said, and the other nodded.

"Then here's the plan . . ." Damian said.

***

They were a few hours outside of Colorado Springs when they saw a fallen tree blocking the road.

"What the hell—" Highway Bill said. He reined in his team and rubbed his grizzled chin with a weathered hand. He had been driving wagons for almost thirty years.

"Take it easy," Shotgun Sam said. "I'll get down and see about moving it."

"You're gonna need help," Bill said.

"And we may get it," Sam said. "Just sit tight and keep your rifle ready."

"You don't think this was an accident?"

"Do you see anywhere that tree could have fallen from and blocked this road?" Sam asked.

Bill squinted and looked, then admitted, "No."

"Then it was put there."

"By who?" Bill asked.

"Whoever it is," Sam said, "they're probably hiding over one of these hills." He pointed to both sides of them. "As soon as I put my hands on that tree, they're going to come running. That's when you grab your rifle, but don't shoot until I do."

"Me?" Bill asked. "I'm a lousy shot."

"Don't worry," Sam said. "Just make some noise and leave the rest to me."

Sam reached beneath the seat, produced a gunbelt and strapped it on, then stepped down from the stage.

Chapter Four

Highway Bill watched as Shotgun Sam walked to the fallen tree and stood staring down at it. He looked to the hills on either side of them, but no one appeared. As he watched, Sam set his shotgun down on the ground, then crouched down to grab hold of the fallen tree

That was when they came.

Two riders from each side appeared and rode down the hills toward them.

"What's happening?" someone from inside the coach called.

"Just stay inside," Bill shouted.

Shotgun Sam stood and looked to both sides but made no move to reclaim his shotgun from the ground. What was he thinking?

Bill picked up his rifle as the riders approached. Two of them stopped next to the coach. The other two rode over to where Shotgun Sam stood.

Bill waited, as he had been told to do.

***

Damian Mair and Albert Lee stopped on either side of Shotgun Sam.

"You're ridin' shotgun?" Damian asked.

"I am."

Damian looked at the shotgun lying in the dirt.

"Seems you put your weapon down," he said.

"So I have."

"We'll be relieving you of your lockbox and your passengers of their valuables."

"I don't think so," Sam said. Instead of spewing a stream of tobacco juice, this time he spit the entire wad from his mouth. "I'm going to need you to drop your guns to the ground."

"Is that right?"

"It is."

"And what are you gonna do if we don't?" Al Lee asked.

"I'll have to take action," Sam said. "But I can't let you rob this stage. I need you to give yourselves up and tell me who you're working for."

"What makes you think we're workin' for anybody?" Damian asked.

"Well," Sam said, "I didn't know for sure, but now I can see you're not smart enough to be doing this on your own."

"Damian," Al Lee said, "I think he's callin' us stupid."

"You are stupid," Damian said.

"What?"

"You just told him my name," Damian said. "Now we have to kill 'im."

"But we wuz told not to kill anybody."

"And we weren't gonna, until you said my name," Damian explained.

"Sorry," Al Lee mumbled.

"So there you go," Sam said. "Somebody told you to rob the stage, but don't kill anyone. I need to know who that was."

"You can forget that, shotgunner," Damian said. "I've got no choice but to kill you, and then rob the coach."

"Not a chance."

Damian looked grim as he went for his gun.

The shotgunner drew his holstered weapon more swiftly than any of the men had ever seen and shot Damian from his saddle.

"What the hell—" Al Lee said.

"Don't!" the shotgunner shouted.

But Al Lee didn't heed his warning. He drew his gun, leaving the man no choice but to fire again. The bullet struck Lee in the chest and drove him from his saddle.

Sam heard the shots from behind him and turned quickly. He saw Highway Bill pointing his rifle, and the other mounted men bring their guns to bear on the man.

"Damn!" he swore. He had no choice.

He fired two more times, and both of the remaining robbers flew from their saddles.

He walked back to the coach, saw the passengers with their heads sticking out the windows.

"What's happening?" one of them asked.

"An attempted robbery," Sam said, "but it's over now. Nothing to worry about."

He looked up at Highway Bill, who was staring down at him in something akin to awe.

"What the hell—" he said.

"Are you hit?" Sam asked.

"No."

He walked to the two fallen robbers, checked them and saw that they were dead, then turned back to the wagon.

"I'll get my shotgun," he said, "and then our male passengers can help us move this tree."

"Okay," Bill said "but—"

"But what?"

"How'd you do that?" he asked. "You killed four men, and without your shotgun."

"I never liked shotguns."

"But . . . if you ain't a shotgunner, who are you?"

"Name's Adams," the man said, "Clint Adams."

Chapter Five

Two weeks earlier . . .

Denver was always an enjoyable stop for Clint Adams, especially if his friend, private Detective Talbot Roper, was in town and not away on a case.

He sent Roper a telegram telling him he was coming to town, and they arranged to meet for supper in the dining room of Clint's regular hotel, the Denver House.

"You got here just in time," Roper said, when they were seated at a table.

"Don't tell me, let me guess," Clint said. "You have to leave town."

"And I need your help with another case," the detective said. "There's a stageline that runs between here and Colorado Springs, and they've been robbed several times."

"Anybody get hurt?"

"No," Roper said, "not yet. But I'd like to head this off before somebody does."

"Why don't you tell them to get somebody else if you don't have the time?" Clint asked.

"They're willing to pay a lot of money," Roper said.

"Then let the other case go."

"There's a lot of money in that one, too."

"Is that really the only reason you take these cases?" Clint asked. "For the money?"

"Exactly!"

Clint sighed.

"Okay, give me the details."

"Let's order steaks first," Roper said. "On me, of course."

"Of course!" Clint agreed.

***

He didn't get much in the way of details, except for the fact that the stageline had an office in Denver.

"You can go there tomorrow and get all the pertinent details. Then you can figure out how you want to proceed."

"And what about you?" Clint asked. "Don't you want to know my plans?"

"No," Roper said, "I have complete faith in you."

"That's good to know."

"Just tell them that you're part of my firm, and we'll take the job."

"Am I getting paid for this?"

Roper said. "Just tell me how much."

"I'm not going to take money from you, Tal," Clint said. "I'll go see these people in the morning."

After supper they went to the hotel bar for a couple of beers and some catching up. But eventually they got back to Roper's business.

"I'm heading for New York," he said. "It's a big job that the Pinkertons have already failed at."

"Ah," Clint said, "so you want to show up poor Robert and William."

"They're not the detective their father was," Roper said.

"Allan was one of a kind."

"And a pain in the ass," Roper said.

"A great big pain in the ass," Clint agreed.

They both lifted their beers and said. "To Allan Pinkerton!"

Roper put his mug down empty.

"I'm going to turn in," he said. "I'll be on the first train in the morning to New York."

Clint shook his friend's hand.

"I'll be at the Waldorf in Manhattan," Roper said. "If you've a need to contact me."

"I'll try and get the job done without having to bother you," Clint promised.

Roper left the bar, and Clint ordered another beer.

***

Clint went up to his room, washed himself in the sink, using the hotel's indoor plumbing to do so. It was something he could get used to, but most of the hotels he visited throughout the West were still without it.

He thought about the job Roper had asked him to do. Well, it was more of a favor, and they both knew it was not one he would be able to refuse. The two men owed each other their lives countless times over, and there was no way to tell whose turn it was to collect. So whenever one asked a favor of the other, they simply gave it.

Clint undressed and, even though he was confident in the lock on the door and the inaccessibility of his third floor window, he still hung his holster on the bedpost, out of habit. Then he sat on the bed and reached for the book he was currently reading, something new from a writer named H. Rider Haggard called *KING SOLOMON'S MINES*. He had started it some time ago, and now figured he was going to have to finish it before he left Denver for Colorado Springs. He didn't think he'd have any time to read while he was trying to locate a gang of stagecoach robbers.

Chapter Six

Clint found the offices of the Colorado Stageline on Market Street. When he entered, the woman sitting at the reception desk looked up and smiled.

"Can I help you?"

"I'm Clint Adams," he said. "I'm supposed to have a meeting with a man named . . . Cole?"

"Langdon Cole," she said. "Yes, he runs the company. Can I tell him why—"

"I work . . . with Talbot Roper, the private detective."

"Oh yes, Mr. Roper," she said. "Of course." She stood up. "I'll tell him you're here."

He watched the young woman walk to a door and enter. She was slender, in her twenties, and seemed to glide rather than walk. When she came back out, her smile was even broader.

"Mr. Cole will see you," she said, holding the door for him.

"Thank you."

She closed the door behind him as a man rose from the desk in front of him. He was tall, stout, in his fifties, wearing an expensive suit.

"Mr. Adams, is it?" Cole asked. "Sent by Talbot Roper?"

"That's right."

"Where's Roper?"

"He had to go to New York on another case," Clint said. "He asked me to come and help you."

"Well then," Cole said, "have a seat. Can I have my girl get you something? Coffee?"

"Coffee would be fine," Clint said, even though he had just had breakfast.

Cole walked to the door, opened it, said, "Mary, bring some coffee, please," then returned to his desk.

"Well," he said, folding his hands on top of his desk, "where do we start?"

"Try the beginning," Clint suggested. "When was your first stage held up?"

"Several months ago," Cole said, "when we first opened the office in Colorado Springs."

"Do you have other stage offices?"

"Yes," Cole said, "we have a run between Colorado Springs and Trinidad, Trinidad and Leadville, Leadville and Gunnison, Gunnison and Denver."

"Have there been any robberies on those lines?"

"No."

"All right, then," Clint said, "what did they get?"

"A payroll we were carrying," Cole said.

"And when was the next?"

"A couple of weeks later."

"A payroll, again?"

"No," Cole said, "but we were delivering a lockbox filled with deposits from a bank in Colorado Springs to a bank in Denver."

"So someone knew about the payroll, and the deposits."

"Apparently."

"And then?"

"A third hold up about two weeks ago," Cole said. "We were carrying some valuable certificates for a business here in Denver."

"And could those certificates be turned into cash?" Clint asked.

"That I don't know. Why?"

"They might still be out there," Clint said. "The robbers could be looking for someone to take them off their hands."

"Can you find them?"

"We can try," Clint said. "But I think I should go to Colorado Springs and see your set up there. Who's in charge?"

"We just have a clerk there named . . ." Cole moved some papers around on his desk. At that moment Mary came in with a tray of coffee.

"Mary, what's that clerk's name in Colorado Springs?" Cole asked.

She put the tray down on the desk, handed Clint a cup and said, "That'd be Carl Walker, sir. He's been the clerk there since you opened that office."

"Right, right, Walker," Cole said. "Thank you, Mary."

She nodded and withdrew.

"Where did you find this fella Walker?" Clint asked.

"He came in and applied for the job," Cole said. "We advertised that we'd be opening an office in Colorado Springs. He claimed to know the area and seemed a good fit."

"You trust him?"

"He hasn't given me any reason not to."

"Well . . . I have an idea about how I'd like to handle this, but I'd have to think about it overnight. I'll come back in the morning with a plan. Let's say I'll be going to Colorado Springs by the end of the week."

"Okay."

"Do you have any stages running at the moment?"

"Yes," Cole said, "but they're not carrying anything valuable."

"Then I'll take one of them when I do leave," Clint suggested, standing. "How many stages do you run?"

"We have half a dozen stages running from different towns," Cole said.

"Have any others been robbed."

"No, just the Colorado Springs one."

"I see."

"Can I ask you something, Mr. Adams?" Cole said.

"Sure, go ahead."

"You're the gentleman who is known as the Gunsmith, right?"

"That's right," Clint said. "Is that a problem?"

"No," Cole said, "no problem, at all." They shook hands. "I'll see you tomorrow morning, then."

Chapter Seven

Clint took the day to work out a plan, and then spent the afternoon shopping for it. He bought clothes he wouldn't ordinarily wear, a shotgun he wouldn't usually carry, and then to top it off, he bought a few plugs of tobacco. If you didn't want to be recognized, a wad of chewing tobacco in your cheek could really change the shape of your face.

When he returned to the Denver House with his purchases, he was surprised to find Langdon Cole's girl—Clint didn't know whether she was an assistant or secretary—waiting for him in the lobby.

"Hello, Mr. Adams," she said, rushing up to him.

"Miss . . .?"

"Oh, I'm sorry," she said sticking out her hand, "my name's Mary Preston. I'm Mr. Cole's personal assistant."

"Aren't you a little young for a position like that?" Clint asked.

"I'm not as young as you might think," she said, but offered nothing further.

"I see," he said. "Well, I'm assuming your boss sent you over here?"

"He did."

"Have you had lunch?"

"I haven't, no," she said.

"Neither have I," he said, showing her his purchases, "I've been a little busy. Would you like to have lunch here in the hotel?"

"That would be . . . nice," she said.

"All right," Clint said. "Just let me have a bellman take this stuff up to my room."

He went to the desk, left the packages and asked the clerk to have them taken to his room.

"Yes, sir, right away," the man said.

He returned to where Mary was standing. "All right, now we can have lunch."

They got seated in the dining room, ordered their lunch, and then Clint asked, "So, what brings you here this afternoon, Miss Preston?"

"First of all," she said, with a smile, "I think since we're going to be working together, you should call me Mary . . . Clint."

"Working together?"

"Yes," she said, "you see, I've been after Mr. Cole to give me more responsibilities, and since we only have a clerk in Colorado Springs, I offered to go there with you—"

"Out of the question," he said, cutting her off.

She was undaunted.

"Well, Mr. Cole thought it was a fine idea," she said. "I'm afraid you'll have to take it up with him."

"Miss Preston," Clint said, "just what help do you think you can be to me?"

"I can be someone in authority at the stageline," she said.

"How do you think your clerk is going to feel about that?" Clint asked.

"He's a clerk, Mr. Adams," she said. "He sells tickets. That's all."

"I see."

"Now I hope that arguing about this won't ruin our nice lunch," she said.

"Oh, I doubt that it will," he said, because he intended to argue with her boss, not her.

They ate and had a pleasant conversation, mostly about what had brought her to Denver and gotten her the job she had. Clint preferred not to discuss where he had been or what he had done lately.

After lunch he paid the bill and walked her to the door of the hotel.

"I'll be in tomorrow morning to see your boss," he told her.

"I'll let him know that we talked," she said, and left the hotel.

She was a pleasant young lady, but he doubted she'd be any help to him in Colorado Springs.

***

"I'm afraid I want her to go with you," Cole said, the next morning. "I'll need somebody on-site to keep me informed."

Clint sighed. All right, then, he might as well put her to good use.

"Then she can help me implement my plan," he said. "She can go into the office first and tell the clerk that you've hired someone to ride shotgun."

"The Gunsmith riding shotgun," Cole said. "That should keep robbers away."

"No," Clint said, "I won't be riding shotgun under my own name. After all, we want to find out who's committing these robberies. I'll be there under an assumed name."

"And what would that be?"

Clint thought about the clothes he would be wearing, and the tobacco he was going to chew, and on the spot he came up with, "Shotgun Sammy Slade."

"Really?" Cole asked.

"Can you come up with something better?" Clint asked.

"No, I don't think so," Cole admitted.

"All right then," Clint said, "your girl, Mary, isn't going to be able to travel with me. We don't want to be seen together. And, of course, we won't acknowledge each other on the street."

"I'll let her know."

"Good. In the event I have something to report, I'll tell her, and she can send you a telegram."

"We have a telegraph in the station, so that'll be easy," Cole said.

"I'll probably have her do it in the town's telegraph office," Clint said. "I don't even want your clerk to know who I really am."

"I see," Cole said. "All right, I'll let her know."

"Does she know him?"

"I believe they saw each other the day I hired him, but I wouldn't say they know each other," Cole answered.

"Good," Clint said. "Let's see if we can keep it that way."

"I don't see why you wouldn't trust him," Cole commented.

"When it comes to payrolls being robbed," Clint said, "I don't trust anybody."

Chapter Eight

Clint and Mary Preston sat across from each other on the stage. They exchanged pleasantries with each other, and the one other passenger, a heavyset woman who wanted to talk all the way. If it wasn't for her, they would not have had to keep up any sort of pretense.

When they reached Colorado Springs, Clint disembarked first, then assisted both ladies out of the coach. The heavyset, middle-aged one thanked him with a simpering grin he assumed was meant to be flirtatious. Mary Preston thanked him quickly and entered the stageline office.

Clint picked up his saddlebags and walked to the nearest hotel, The Peak House. He had left Eclipse behind in Denver with a hostler there he had used before and trusted.

He got himself situated in a room, telling the desk clerk he didn't know how long he would be there. He also explained he had a job with the stageline, and he did it with a wad of tobacco in his cheek. When he got to his room, the first thing he did was spit it out. He hated the taste.

He wanted to give Mary Preston some time with the clerk, so he left his room and went to the saloon that was attached to the hotel. He had a beer to wash the taste of the tobacco from his mouth. He decided to chew a smaller wad as his disguise.

He was on his second beer when Mary Preston appeared at the connecting doorway from the hotel lobby. She looked in, saw him, then turned and walked away. He walked to the door and watched her check in at the desk. When the clerk gave her a key she turned, glanced at Clint, then went to the stairs.

Clint finished his beer, left the empty mug on the bar and walked to the front desk.

"The lady who just checked in," he said, handing the clerk a dollar. "What room is she in?"

"Room eight, sir," the clerk said, pocketing the dollar, "just down the hall from you."

"Thanks."

Clint went up the stairs, walked down the hall and knocked on the door of room eight. She opened it immediately.

"Come in, quickly," she said. "Before somebody sees you."

He slipped in, and she locked the door.

"You don't want a man seen coming into your room?" he asked.

"Not you," she said. "We're not to be seen together, isn't that right?"

"That's right," he said, "or, not until I start working for the stageline. Did you tell the clerk about me?"

"Yes, Carl's expecting you."

"Today?"

"This afternoon."

"Okay, good," Clint said. "I might as well go over there now. I'll get my shotgun."

"Do you need it?"

"It's part of my disguise."

She smiled.

"Like the tobacco?"

"Yes," he said, making a face. "Terrible tasting stuff, but yes, it makes a good disguise."

"Don't forget," she said, "the clerk's name is Carl Walker."

"Wait," he said. "You know him, don't you?"

"What?"

"You said Carl's waiting for me," Clint said, "as if you knew him."

"I . . . met him in Denver," she admitted.

"And got to know him?"

Her eyes flicked around the room.

"Well, yes—I mean, no, not well. We just . . ."

She looked away and blushed and he knew what she meant.

"Ah, I get it now," he said.

"It was just a . . . one time thing."

"And yet you got your boss to send you here so you could see him."

"I . . . just wanted to help."

"Well, we'll see if you're going to be any help or just add to the problem."

He left the room and headed for the stageline office.

Chapter Nine

Clint entered the stageline office, carrying his shotgun, chewing his tobacco, hunching his shoulders for just a little more disguise.

The man behind the counter was in his thirties, pleasant looking if not handsome. He would certainly appeal to the ladies when they came in.

"Afternoon, sir," the man said.

"You Carl Walker?" Clint asked, using his Shotgun Sam voice.

"I am."

"I'm Sam Slade."

"Our hired shotgun," Walker said. "Welcome. I guess you're the one who's going to keep our stages from bein' robbed."

"That's what I'm gettin' paid for," Clint said.

"Well, you'll have your chance tomorrow morning," Walker said. "Stage is leaving at eight a.m. All you've got to do is be here."

"I can do that."

"You carry a shotgun and wear a sidearm?" Carl Walker asked.

"The holster will go under the seat," Clint said, "just in case. But I figure to do my job with this beauty." He held up his shotgun.

Clint looked around the interior of the office. It had only been built a few years before, and it seemed that Carl Walker kept it fairly clean. In one corner sat the telegraph key.

"You got anythin' to tell me about whose been robbin' these stagecoaches?" Clint asked.

"If I knew that, we wouldn't need you, would we?" Walker asked. "I'd just tell the sheriff."

"Good point."

"That reminds me," Walker said. "You better check in with the law, tell 'im you're here."

"What's his name?"

"Goes by John C. Maybe," Walker said. "Insists on the 'C.' Been the law here for about fifteen years. You can do that today, since we don't need you til tomorrow."

"Gotcha," Clint said.

"And do me a favor?" Walker said.

"What's that?"

"Try not to spit that juice in the office," Walker said. "I like to keep this place clean."

"Gotcha," Clint said, and left.

***

Clint had two options. He could stop in and see the sheriff as Clint Adams, or as Shotgun Sam Slade. He decided since he didn't know the man, to stick to his Sam Slade persona, which was also the way he had signed the register at the hotel. That kept Mary Preston as the only person in town who knew who he really was.

He found the sheriff's office and entered. The man seated behind the desk looked at him with surprise on his heavily lined face. He had a bushy head of grey hair that was going off in every direction.

"Well, well," he said, "I don't get many visitors, anymore. Not since the new police department opened."

"No, don't tell me," Clint said, as Shotgun Sam. "I hate those places."

"Stranger, you just made a friend," the man said. "Have a seat and tell me what brings you here."

Clint sat across from the man.

"You're the sheriff, right?"

"That's right," the man said. "John C. Maybe, at your service."

"My name is Sam Slade," Clint said. "They call me Shotgun Sam. I've been hired to ride shotgun on the Colorado stage."

"Yeah, I figured somethin' like that would happen," Maybe said. "They been hit . . . what? Three times?"

"Yup."

"Well," Maybe said. "Could be you'll be the answer."

"I hope so," Clint said. "I just wanted to tell you that I'll be around for a while."

"Where you stayin'?"

"The Peak House," Clint said. "It's just the closest to the stage office."

"Makes sense."

Clint stood up.

"You any good with that shotgun?" the lawman asked.

"How good do you have to be with a Greener?" Clint asked, and the two men laughed.

"Come by the Starlight Saloon later," Maybe said, "I'll buy you a beer to welcome you to town."

"You going to tell me you don't have a bottle of whiskey in your desk?"

"I do," Maybe said, with a grin, "but I don't share that with anybody."

"I hear that," Clint said. "I'll see you at the saloon."

He left the office, thinking the sheriff wasn't such a bad guy.

Chapter Ten

Normally Clint would've killed time having a beer or two in a saloon. But in this case, he would've been killing time til he had a beer with Sheriff Maybe in the Starlight Saloon. He didn't want to already be drunk when the sheriff arrived, and killed the time in his room, cleaning his revolver and his shotgun. Given that three robberies had already occurred, the weapons were likely to be pressed into service at some point, and he wanted to make sure they were in good working order.

When he finally decided to saunter over to the Starlight, he got there ahead of the lawman and ordered a beer for himself at the bar. The place was pretty busy, since it seemed to offer everything a man could want in a saloon, like girls, gambling, and beer. There was a slanted window above the bar, which allowed customers to look up at the stars, hence the name: Starlight Saloon.

"You're a stranger in town," the bartender said.

"That's right," Clint said. "Just got in today. Name's Sam Slade."

"Plan on stayin' a while?" the middle-aged barkeep asked.

"Might," Clint said, "got me a job ridin' shotgun for the stageline."

"That a fact?" the bartender said. "You heard they been robbed three times in the past coupla months?"

"That's why they hired me, and that's why I took the job," Clint said.

"You have any trouble with the law?" the bartender asked.

"No. Why do you ask?"

"The sheriff just walked in and he's headed this way."

"I met him earlier today," Clint said. "He said he was going to buy me a beer, so get 'em up."

"Right away."

As the lawman walked toward the bar, exchanging greetings along the way, the bartender set two fresh beers on the bar.

"Hey, Sheriff," he greeted.

"Mike," Sheriff Maybe said. "Looks like you met my new friend, Sam."

"We were just gettin' to names," the bartender said, extending his hand. "Mike."

"Sam."

They shook hands, and then he moved down the bar to serve some new customers.

"So," Maybe asked, did you take a look around town?"

"A short walk," Clint said. "Not enough to see the whole town."

"That'll take a while," Maybe said. "We've almost doubled in size in the past seven years."

"I suppose that's why they decided on the modern police station?"

Maybe nodded.

"I had three deputies seven years ago. Now I have none."

"That doesn't seem right, with the population doubling," Clint said.

"My job mostly consists of serving eviction notices or citing people for what their dogs do. The real crimes are handled by the police."

"Have they done anything about the robberies?"

"According to the chief of police, the robberies have taken place outside the city limits."

"You mean he hasn't sent anyone out to where they happened?"

"Not yet," Maybe said, "and I can't get a posse up. People just laugh at me and shake their heads when I try."

"I'd go out with you," Clint said.

"It may come to that," Maybe said, "if there's another robbery and you can't stop it. At least you might see somethin' helpful."

"I'll keep my eyes open, whatever happens," Clint said.

"When's your first ride?" Maybe asked.

"Tomorrow morning."

"What's the stage carryin'?"

"Supposedly nothing of value," Clint said.

"Then maybe you'll make it to Denver and back with no problem."

"We'll see."

"It's only your first ride," he pointed out. "It can happen any time."

"I'll be ready," Clint said.

Maybe finished his beer and set the empty mug down.

"I'm gonna make my rounds."

"You still doing that?" Clint asked.

"Some habits are hard to break," Maybe said. "The sun goes down and I feel like I have to jiggle doors to make sure they're locked."

"The whole town?"

John C. Maybe laughed.

"The part that was here seven years ago," Maybe said. "That's my part."

"Okay, then," Clint said. "See you later, Sheriff."

On his way to the door, the lawman stopped and turned back.

"My friends, even my new friends," he said, "call me John C."

"See you later, John C."

Chapter Eleven

The next morning Clint rose early, had breakfast as Shotgun Sam Slade, and then went to the stage office.

"Good-mornin'," Carl Walker greeted as he walked in. "Are you ready?"

"I'm ready," Clint said.

"Good. You can go out and meet the driver, help him stow bags up top."

Clint saw a couple of people seated on a bench against the wall in the office, assumed they were passengers. He went outside and saw a grizzled old-timer with a large belly struggling with some bags.

"Let me give you a hand," he called.

The man stopped and turned.

"You the new shotgun?"

"That's me," he said. "Shotgun Sam."

"They call me Highway Bill," the driver said. The two men shook hands.

"I'll go up top and you toss the bags up," Clint suggested.

"Sounds like a plan."

They got the bags secured on top of the coach and then Clint dropped down. After that, he held the coach door open for the boarding passengers, assisted the one middle-aged female, who didn't bother to thank him.

Clint climbed up next to Highway Bill, and asked, "Isn't there a stage that leaves here for Trinidad?"

"Yeah," Bill said, "the driver's name is Paddy O'Shea. That one leaves a half hour before we do."

"Every day?"

"None of us have runs every day," Bill said. "In the days we're both scheduled, they leave first."

"Why?"

"Our run is seventy miles," Bill said, "theirs is over a hundred and twenty."

"Got it. Thanks."

Highway Bill snapped the reins. "Here we go!"

***

Clint's first week as Shotgun Sam Slade was uneventful. At no time were they even approached by riders from any direction. It was possible the word had gone out about the shotgun.

He learned that there was about three hours between stage stops, where they'd change teams, maybe get coffee or a meal for the passengers. Some of the runs included an overnight stop, unless Bill wanted to push.

He had gotten into the habit of meeting Sheriff John C. Maybe at the Starlight for a beer each night he was in town. Some nights even a steak. If Highway Bill and he were stopped somewhere along the way, or even in Denver, they would share a meal and get to know each other better. Bill had a long history of driving wagons. Clint had to make up a history for Shotgun Sam, so he stole a little of it from other people, specifically some Calamity Jane stories he hoped the old coachman wouldn't already have heard.

As the second week started, "Shotgun Sam" had not become friends with the clerk, Carl Walker. And Clint hadn't seen much of Mary Preston during that time either. That was all right with him, but he couldn't help wondering if she had been seeing the clerk on the side.

At the end of the second week, Clint met the sheriff at the Tenderloin Steakhouse.

"John C.," he said, joining the man at a back table.

They ordered steak and beer.

"Here's to two weeks with no robberies," Maybe said, lifting his beer. "I guess you scared them all off."

"Yeah, right. We'll find out tomorrow."

"What's tomorrow?"

"Well, after two weeks of no robberies, we're going to be carrying a lockbox with a payroll in it."

"Have you told anybody else besides me?" Maybe asked.

"No," Clint said, "only you."

"That's bad."

"Why?"

"If you do get robbed," Maybe said, "you're gonna think I talked. Or worse, that I set it up."

"You know what, John C.?" Clint said. "I trust you, which is why I told you."

"Okay, then," Maybe said. "That's good to know."

While they ate, they talked about what John C. was going to do when he was done wearing a badge.

"And when will that be?" Clint asked.

"Probably at the end of this term," Maybe said. "That would give me a few months."

"Hopefully they'll be a quiet three months," Clint said.

"That'd be nice."

***

Mary Preston had been sleeping with Carl Walker every night since arriving in Colorado Springs. But on this night, he told her he couldn't be with her.

"I've got things to do," he explained.

Like have sex with Amanda, and meet with his men, Damian Mair, and Al Lee, to solidify the plan to rob the stage, and then go back to Amanda.

In the morning he was at the office when Highway Bill stuck his head in and nodded.

"Okay, folks," he said, "time to board."

***

Outside, Clint got up top to catch the bags Bill was tossing him, and to make sure the lockbox containing the payroll was, indeed, locked and secure.

Shotgun Sammy dropped down from the top of the stage and spit a stream of brown tobacco juice into the dirt.

"Ready to go?" he asked Highway Bill.

"Yeah, we're ready," Bill said. "Let's climb aboard."

The two men climbed atop the stage, and Highway Bill picked up the reins and put his hand on the brake.

"Hopefully," he said, "we don't get robbed, today."

Shotgun Sammy spat a stream of tobacco and said, "That's what we're hoping for."

Bill released the brake and shook the reins at the team.

Chapter Twelve

The day of the robbery . . .

The stage rode back into Colorado Springs with the bodies of four would be-robbers lashed to the top, next to the lockbox.

As it pulled up in front of the office, some people gathered round, and Carl Walker came out of the office.

"What happened?" he asked.

"Four men tried to hold us up," Highway Bill said, looking down at the clerk.

"And?"

"And Shotgun Sam got 'em."

"All of 'em?" Walker asked.

"All four," Bill said, "dead. I guess you better send somebody for the law, and then make arrangements for these passengers to have tickets on tomorrow's stage."

"Yeah," Walker said, "I guess I better."

Highway Bill turned in his seat and looked at Clint.

"I guess you wanna keep bein' Shotgun Sam for a while, huh?"

"I think that would be best, Bill."

"Well," the driver said, "you saved my ass, so I guess yer entitled to be called whatever you want."

"Hey, Sam!"

Clint turned and looked down at the ground on his right, saw Sheriff Maybe standing there.

"Looks like you had to do your job," the lawman said.

"I sure did, Sheriff."

"Well," Maybe said, "the police should be here soon. You can tell them the whole story."

"What about you?" Clint asked.

"You can tell me the story later, over a steak."

"You got it."

By the time Bill and Clint had dropped down and let the passengers out, a couple of uniformed policemen had arrived. First the two young lawmen got the story from Bill, and then listened to Clint's version. Meanwhile, the passengers complained at Carl Walker—except for Amanda, who was envisioning another night with the handsome young clerk.

Eventually, another policeman arrived, and the two young officers stood at attention.

"Well," Carl Walker said, "what brings you out, Chief?"

"I heard about the robbery," the older man said, "thought I'd come and have a look."

"Well, you already know Highway Bill," Walker said. "This is our shotgun, Sam Slade. Slade, this is

Chief Ed Dillon, of the new Colorado Springs Police Department."

The two men shook hands.

"I heard these robberies were outside your jurisdiction," Clint said.

"Well, that's what I came to find out," Chief Dillon said. "Where'd it happen?"

Clint looked at Highway Bill.

"As usual," the driver said, "outside the city limits."

"Not much we can do, then," Dillon said. "Did they hurt anybody?"

"There was shootin'," Bill said, "but Slade, here, took care of 'em."

"All of them?" the Chief asked.

"I got lucky," Clint said.

"Weren't no luck," Bill said, but then he turned away when Clint gave him a look.

"Where are the bodies?" Dillon asked.

"The clerk arranged for them to be taken to the undertaker's," Clint said.

"Guess the least I can do is go over and have a look, see if I know them," Dillon said.

"Yeah," Clint said, "maybe that'd be helpful."

As the Chief walked away, Bill turned to Clint and asked, "How about a drink?"

"I'll need a report from the two of you, first," Carl Walker said. "Then I'll have to send it to Denver."

"You got any whiskey in the office?" Bill asked.

"I don't keep liquor around," Walker said. "You can go and have your drink after we're done."

Walker reentered the office with Clint and Highway Bill following.

***

Later that evening, Clint met Sheriff Maybe at the Tenderloin.

"I went over to the undertakers to have a look," Maybe said, after they'd ordered.

"Run into the chief there?" Clint asked.

"No, I waited til he was gone," Maybe said. "According to the undertaker, our chief didn't recognize any of the men."

"But you did, didn't you?" Clint asked.

"That's right I did," Maybe said, "Fella named Al Lee."

"Why would he be robbing the stage?" Clint asked. "Is that the kind of thing he did?"

"He did whatever he was hired to do," Maybe said.

"So somebody hired him to do it."

"I'd say so," Maybe said. "Too bad he's dead and can't say who."

Chapter Thirteen

Clint gave it some thought while he and John C. Maybe were finishing their meal. If he trusted the man, then he might as well trust him all the way. So he came to a decision.

When they got pie and coffee for dessert, Clint said, "John C., I've got something to tell you."

"Is it gonna surprise me?"

"I think so."

"Do I need somethin' stronger to drink?"

"Maybe later."

"Okay, then," Maybe said. "Let me have it."

"My name is not Shotgun Sam Slade," Clint said.

"Really?" Maybe asked. "That's the surprise?"

"You knew?"

"I figured."

"How?"

"The chewin' tobacco," Maybe said. "It was a little too much."

"Disgusting stuff," Clint said.

"It showed," Maybe said. "So, now the surprise part is when you tell me your real name? The part I'll need a drink for?" The lawman laughed. "Your real name's Wild Bill Hickok?"

"Clint Adams," Clint said.

Maybe stopped laughing and stared for a moment. Then he said, "Pretty much the same thing."

"Not even close."

"That's not what most people would say," Maybe commented. "A legend is a legend."

"I'm not here as a legend," Clint said. "I was asked by a friend to look into these robberies and try to stop them."

"It looks like you did that."

"Not if they were hired," Clint said. "Chances are they'll just hire somebody else to do it next time."

"Next time?" Maybe asked. "Like tomorrow? Are you takin' that lockbox again tomorrow?"

"I don't know," Clint said. "I'll have to talk to that ticket clerk. But I doubt they'd get someone hired in time to try again tomorrow."

"I agree. You're probably pretty safe for a while."

"I suppose I'll have to go down to the office early tomorrow morning to find out."

John C. Maybe sat back in his chair and regarded Clint critically.

"So you're the Gunsmith."

"That's right."

"You any good with that shotgun?"

"I can use it," Clint said, "but I did all the damage with my Peacemaker."

"I wondered about that when I saw the four bodies, and none of them had been torn up by buckshot."

"I actually would have liked to take at least one man alive," Clint said, "But I couldn't be choosy with four of them shooting at me."

When they finished their meal, they each paid their bill and then stopped out in front of the restaurant.

"Beer?" Maybe asked.

"I'll meet you at the Starlight later," Clint said. "Maybe I can catch the clerk at the office now and find out if we're heading out again tomorrow."

"I'll see you there."

They walked off in separate directions.

***

Clint entered the office and found the ticket clerk at his desk.

"What brings you back at this time?" Carl Walker asked. "I should've locked the door."

"I wanted to find out if we're taking that lockbox tomorrow," Clint said.

"Why not?" Walker asked. "I doubt they'll try again so soon."

"So you think they will try again?"

"Sure," Walker said, "and there'll probably be six of 'em next time, so they can handle you."

"Did you send your reports to Denver?"

"I did."

"Any word back?"

"They said to congratulate you on stopping the robberies."

"Are they sending anyone else?"

"They didn't say."

"Well then," Clint said, "I'll see you early tomorrow."

"Make sure that shotgun of yours is loaded," Walker said, "just in case."

"Good-night," Clint said, and left. He walked slowly through the street to the Starlight and as he entered, didn't see Sheriff Maybe there, yet. Mike the bartender had a beer waiting for him.

"Heard you had some excitement," he said. "This one's on the house."

"Why's that?" Clint asked.

"I like when my customers don't get killed."

Chapter Fourteen

Clint was on his second beer when John C. Maybe walked in.

By the time he got to the bar, Mike had a beer there waiting.

"That one's on me," Clint said.

"Thanks," Maybe said. "You headin' out tomorrow?"

"We are," Clint said.

"Any extra help?"

"I was thinking of getting Highway Bill a shotgun."

"Can he use one?"

"Can you miss with one?" Clint asked.

"I guess you're gonna find out."

"Probably not tomorrow, though," Clint said. "At least, I hope not. I'm not looking forward to killing men two days in a row."

"So maybe next time," Maybe said, "you'll get that live one you want."

"I'll give it a try," Clint promised.

"All you've got to do is prove that the robbery plans are originatin' from here," Maybe said, "and the Chief will have to do somethin'."

"Can he do anything?" Clint asked. "I mean, does he know his job?"

"Who knows?" Maybe said, with a shrug. "They hired him from back East, but I haven't seen him actually do anythin', yet."

"What about you?" Clint asked.

"What about me?"

"Don't you want to do something during your last three months on the job?" Clint asked. "Don't you want to prove to everybody you shouldn't be retiring?"

"How do I do that?"

"Like you said," Clint replied, "maybe we can prove that the robberies are being planned here, in Colorado Springs."

"I'm not supposed to do that kind of thing."

"But the new police aren't doing anything," Clint reminded him. "All you'd have to do is use some of the contacts you've built up over the years. If somebody around here is trying to hire men to rob the stage—"

"Okay, okay, I get it," Maybe said, cutting him off. "I guess if you're out there riskin' your life on the stage, the least I can do is ask some questions here in town."

"Good," Clint said, "then we're working together on this, John C."

"I guess we are," the lawman said.

***

Clint answered the knock at his door that night with gun in hand. It was Mary Preston. He let her in and holstered his gun. He was still wearing his Levi's and shirt, with the buttons undone and his boots off. Mary was wearing a simple dress.

"What brings you here?" he asked. "We haven't seen each other very much the past two weeks."

"That's why," she said. "I wanted to check in with you, especially after what happened today. Is it all over?"

"Not even close."

"Why not?" she asked. "You killed the stage robbers, didn't you?"

"I did," Clint said, "but we don't know who hired them."

"Hired them?"

"Yes," Clint said, "somebody's behind this, Mary. There's no guarantee that when we go out tomorrow, we won't be stopped, again."

"Do you really think that will happen?"

"Honestly, no, not tomorrow," Clint said, "but yes, somewhere down the road, it'll happen again. So no, it's not over."

"Oh." She looked disappointed.

"Did you send your boss a telegram telling him it was done?" he asked.

"I sent him a telegram explaining to him what happened," she said. "I didn't draw any conclusion."

"And the clerk, Walker, he sent his report to Denver," Clint said. "I haven't heard anything from your boss, so I assume I'm still on the payroll."

"Yes," she said, "I haven't received any instructions to terminate you."

"Then send him another telegram," Clint said. "Tell him I said it's not over."

"A-all right."

"And then you can go on sleeping with your ticket clerk," Clint said.

"What?" she said. "How did you—"

"Never mind," he said. "It's not important. What you do on your own time is your own business."

"I—he's not—I wasn't with him last night," she said, "and probably won't be tonight."

"That's between you and him," Clint told her. "I'm going to do a little more reading, and then turn in so I can get up early."

"And I'll send another telegram tomorrow," she promised.

"Good," he said. "Then get some sleep tonight."

"Yes," she said, "yes, I will."

She left and moments later he heard her door open and close.

Chapter Fifteen

When Clint got to the stageline office, the three passengers from the day before were there, plus two more—a woman and a small boy. Clint didn't like the idea of a child being on a stage that might be robbed, but he really didn't think the mastermind of the robberies could have gotten the whole thing set up again, so soon.

"'mornin'," the clerk, Carl Walker, greeted him.

"Good-morning."

"I think Bill's out back hitchin' up the horses," Walker said. "Wanna give him a hand?"

"Sure thing."

Clint went out the back door and saw Bill struggling with the team.

"Hang on, there," Clint said. "Let me help you."

Bill looked around, saw who was speaking, and then said, "Oh, thanks . . . Sam."

Together they got the four-horse team hitched to the stagecoach, drove it around front and began loading it up. The last thing Clint did up top was lash down the lockbox. Then he dropped down to assist the passengers into the coach, specifically the women and the child.

"Mister, are we gonna get robbed today?" the boy asked.

"I don't think so, son," he replied.

"Aw, shucks!" the boy said.

"Joey, hush," his mother said. She looked at Clint and said, "He heard about the robbery yesterday, and now he's been looking forward to it."

"I think we'll be fine, ma'am," he told her.

"Are you the man who foiled the robbery?" she asked.

"I am, yes," he said. "And if it comes to that, I'll do it again today."

"Thank you," she said, as he closed the door.

"Are we ready?" Highway Bill asked from his seat.

"Everybody's aboard," Clint assured him.

"Then get your ass up here and let's get goin'," Bill said.

Clint climbed up and sat next to Bill, who shook the reins at the team. The clerk, Walker, watched them from the doorway.

The previous day, Clint had stowed his gunbelt beneath his seat. Today he was holding his shotgun and wearing his sidearm.

"Denver or bust!" Bill shouted, as they started off.

***

They made it to Denver safely, which caused little Joey to disembark wearing a disappointed pout. Bill had pushed to make the trip without resting at a stage stop overnight.

Highway Bill dropped down to the ground gratefully heaving a sigh of relief.

"Let's get everything unloaded and start back," he told Clint.

"Tonight?"

"I don't wanna stay in Denver," Bill said. "There's a stopover just about an hour or so out of town. We can spend the night there and change the team." Most of the stage stops were about fifteen miles apart, which meant the teams put in about three hours a day pulling the coach. If he wanted to get an hour out of Denver and stop, that was up to him.

"You're the driver," Clint said.

They got everything off the top of the stage, including the lockbox, which they turned over to the proper people, then climbed back on board.

When they reached the stopover an hour out, Clint realized Bill had wanted to stop there because he was friends with the middle-aged couple who ran it, Tom and Ginny Shackelford.

He introduced Clint as "Sam Slade," and assured him that the woman was a great cook. As it turned out, Clint had the best bowl of beef stew he'd ever had, and he said so.

"That's very kind of you," Ginny said. "Will you have some more?"

"Definitely!"

She gave him another bowl and another piece of crusty bread to soak it up with. Highway Bill and Tom were chattering away while they ate, things only old friends could talk about, so Clint remained silent and enjoyed the food.

"Sam!"

Clint realized Bill was talking to him.

"Oh, yeah, what?"

"You can sleep on that cot in the corner," Tom said. "Ginny will give you a blanket."

"That's fine."

"I'll be in the other corner," Bill said. "We'll get an early start."

"After a good breakfast," Ginny added, sternly.

"You won't get any argument from me," Clint told her.

**

Clint bedded down on his cot, while Bill and Tom continued to sit at the table and talk over coffee. The smell of the coffee finally drew him, and he sat with them and drank it for half the night. Luckily Ginny had prepared a huge pot before turning in herself.

"So Sam," Tom asked, "you really expect the stage to be hit again?"

"I do," Clint said. "I figure the men I killed were hired hands."

"If that's true," Tom said, "there'll be more."

"Yeah, I figured that, too," Clint agreed.

"Well," Tom said, "I hope your luck stays good."

"Believe me," Highway Bill said, "this man don't need luck," but he fell silent when Clint gave him a quick look.

Chapter Sixteen

During the ride back to Colorado Springs, Clint said to Bill, "You've got to be careful what you say to people."

"I know Tom a long time, and he ain't even in Denver or Colorado Springs . . . but I get it. I'll keep my big trap shut."

"Bill, how well do you know Carl Walker?" Clint asked.

"Not that good," Bill said. "He keeps to himself . . . except for women."

"Yeah, I got that feeling about him."

"You know that lady who was a passenger when we got robbed," Bill said. "I seen Walker comin' out of her hotel the night before."

"I thought he and Mary Preston had something going on," Clint said.

"Yeah, he's been seein' her since you and her got here," Bill said. "But that don't mean he's gonna miss an easy chance, and that lady passenger, she was kinda lonely. Almost twenty years older than Mary, but kinda lonely, which made her an easy target for a man like Walker."

"So I get the feeling you don't like him much," Clint said.

"He's a . . . whataya call animals who hunt?"

"A predator?"

"That's it," Bill said. "He's a predator, so that makes two reasons I don't like 'im."

"What's the other one?"

"He treats me like shit!"

***

When Clint and Bill got back to Colorado Springs, they parted company at the stage office. Bill walked the animals and stage behind the office, where he'd unhitch the team and clean the stage. Clint decided to go inside and talk with Carl Walker, just to get a feel for the man.

"Made it there and back without firing a shot," he told the clerk.

"Took your time getting back," Walker said.

"Did we have a run today?"

"No," Walker said, "tomorrow morning."

"So we visited with Tom and Ginny Shackelford," Clint said. "Nice people, and she's a great cook."

"As I recall," Walker said, "she's got a face like a mule."

"She may not be a beauty, but she ain't that bad," Clint commented.

"That's your opinion," Walker said. "Look, I've got to close up."

"I get it," Clint said. "You're not the friendly type."

"You're right," Walker said. "You get it."

Clint left and Carl Walker locked the door behind him.

***

Clint was about to enter the sheriff's office when the door opened, and the lawman came walking out.

"John C. Maybe," Clint said.

"Shotgun Sam," Maybe said, with a smile. "Or are you usin' your real name today?"

"Shotgun's good," Clint said.

"I guess you made it yesterday without any trouble."

"Yes."

"So now what?"

"So now I continue to ride shotgun until it happens again," Clint said.

"And what if it doesn't happen again?"

"What do you mean?"

"Walk with me," Maybe said. "I mean, what if you scared them off and they don't try to rob another stage?"

"Not very likely," Clint said.

"Why not?" Maybe asked. "What if they decide to take their business somewhere else?"

"That would be a good thing," Clint admitted, "but I still doubt it. They're not about to let one man chase them away from their playground."

They passed the Starlight Saloon, which was fairly busy. But neither made a move to go inside. It was only seventy miles from Denver to Colorado Springs, and by spending the night at the stagecoach stopover they were even closer, so they had reached Colorado Springs by evening. But it wasn't time for either of them to go inside.

"I've got some papers to serve," Maybe told Clint. "I'll see you in the Starlight later."

"All right," Clint said. "I'm going to have a bath, and then maybe a nap. I didn't really sleep all that well last night."

"Why's that?"

"I slept on a cot that was worse than the ones in your cells."

Chapter Seventeen

When Clint got to his hotel, he approached the front desk to arrange for a bath.

"Right away, sir," the clerk said. "Too bad we don't have indoor facilities, huh?"

"It's not important," Clint said. "I'll be right back down for the bath."

As he started up the stairs the clerk said, "Oh, Mr. Slade."

"Yeah?"

"Chief Dillon was here earlier, lookin' for you," the clerk said. "He told me to let you know you should stop in and see him."

"All right," Clint said, "after my hot bath."

"Yes sir," the clerk said. "Right away, sir."

Clint went up to his room to get some fresh clothes.

***

After soaking in a hot bath until it wasn't hot, anymore, Clint got dressed and left the hotel. He didn't know where the new police station building was, so he flagged down a horse-drawn cab and told the driver, "The police station, please."

"Yes, sir," the driver said.

It was only about fifteen minutes later when they pulled up in front of a new two-story brick building.

"If I was you, I'd watch it in there," the young driver said to Clint as he stepped down.

"Why's that?" Clint asked.

"I heard that everything in that building ain't on the up-and-up."

"Thanks for the warning," Clint said. "I'll keep that in mind."

Although he had done away with the tobacco part of his disguise, Clint still had a sour taste in the back of his throat as he approached the front door. It could have just been his dislike of these modern police stations. The new decade was still more than ten years away, and Clint could feel himself walking a fine line between the old West and the twentieth century. As far as he was concerned, these new law enforcement departments were on the wrong side.

As he entered, he saw that the lobby featured a large front desk, the type he had seen before. Behind the desk was a man in uniform with three stripes on his arm.

"Can I do somethin' for you?" the sergeant asked, looking at him sourly.

"Yes," Clint said, "you can tell Chief Dillon that Sam Slade is here to see him."

"Yeah?" the man said. "And why would I do that?"

"Because I'm here at his request."

The man had a lantern jaw, which he firmed for a moment, then growled, "Wait here, I'll let 'im know you're here."

The sergeant left the desk. Moments later a different officer, with no stripes, came and took his place, and just after that Chief Dillon appeared.

"Thanks for dropping by," he said, shaking Clint's hand. "Let's talk."

Dillon headed for the door.

"Where are we going?" Clint asked. "Don't you have an office?"

"I don't want to talk here," Dillon said. "There's a place I like a few blocks away. Come on, I'll buy you a drink."

***

Clint let Dillon lead him to a place called Ruth's Café. Judging from the name, Clint expected some kind of flowery interior, but instead he got dark wood and gold railings.

"Why is this place called 'Ruth's'?" he asked.

"The guy who owns it is named Ruth," Dillon told him, "Andy Ruth. He's from back East, got here around the same time I did."

They got a table in a darkened corner and Dillon ordered two beers.

"Before the waiter gets back," Dillon said, "are you hungry? They serve food here, and it's where I usually have supper around this time."

"I could eat," Clint said.

"They have a great venison steak."

"Sounds good."

When the waiter came with their drinks, Dillon ordered two venison steak plates.

"Comin' up, Chief."

"He knows you're the chief," Clint said.

"Yeah, but don't worry, I pay for all my meals here," Dillon said. "And I like it because none of my men ever come in here. They have their own place right across the street."

"I saw it," Clint said. He'd spotted McNulty's as he entered the police station, figured it was an Irish saloon the police would probably frequent.

"Yeah," Dillon said, "my men have their place and I have mine."

"While we're waiting for our food," Clint said, "maybe you can tell me why you wanted to see me."

"Sure," Dillon said, "I was just hoping you'd tell me what the Gunsmith was doing in Colorado Springs under the name Shotgun Sam Slade?"

Chapter Eighteen

Clint didn't bother denying it.

"How'd you know?"

"It's my job to know," Dillon said. "I recognized you as soon as I saw you. Plus, you looked real uncomfortable with that mouthful of tobacco."

"Why didn't you say anything?"

"I wanted to see what you were up to," Dillon told him.

"So why let the cat out of the bag now?" Clint asked.

"Well, now that I know what you're up to," Dillon said. "I want to know what your future plans are."

"That's simple," Clint said. "I'm going to find out who's behind the stage holdups and put a stop to them."

"You don't think you've done that already?" Chief Dillon asked.

"No," Clint said, "I just killed some hirelings. There'll be more."

"And you think they'll come from here, in Colorado Springs?"

"It's possible," Clint said. "Probably likely."

"How are you going to find out?"

"I've got somebody keeping their ears open."

"Somebody with contacts?"

"Definitely," Clint said.

"Well, I know it's not one of my men, so it must be Sheriff Maybe."

Clint didn't respond right away. Their food came but they continued to talk while they ate.

"You know he's done in this town, right? He's got maybe three months left on his term."

"So I heard, but he's a man who seems to know his job."

"You mean serving papers?"

"I mean upholding the law," Clint said. "You could do worse than hiring him for your department."

"He's an old dog," Dillon said. "I don't think I'm going to be able to teach him any new tricks."

"He might be able to teach your men a thing or two," Clint said.

"Never mind him," Dillon said. "I want you to keep in touch with me and let me know what you find."

"You've made it pretty clear you don't think these robberies are yours to handle."

"Maybe you'll find out something that will change my mind?" Dillon said. "All I'm asking is that you keep me informed."

"I think I can do that, Chief."

"Good. How's the meal?"

"Like you said," Clint replied, "very good venison steak."

***

Clint found John C. Maybe standing with a beer. By the time he got to the bar, Mike the bartender had set one up for him.

"What's been goin' on?" Maybe asked.

Clint told him about his meal with the chief of police.

"So he knew who you were when he saw you?"

"He did."

"Why didn't he say something then?"

"He wanted to see what I was up to and make sure I know that he's on to me."

"There are lots of people usin' names that ain't their own," the lawman said. "Not necessarily his business."

"What about you?" Clint asked. "You got another name?"

"Oh no," the lawman said, "I'm still John C. Maybe. But now I can call you Clint, instead of Shotgun Sam."

"Just not in public," Clint said. "I'd still like to keep it quiet."

"I don't blame you," Maybe said. "Although, don't you think it would've been helpful to let it be known the Gunsmith was riding shotgun on the stage?"

"For some," Clint said, "for others it would've been a challenge."

"I get that," Maybe said. "It might've brought more stage robbers out of the cornfields."

"This way I think I still have a chance to find out who's behind the robberies."

"And that's your job, right?"

"Actually," Clint said, "I'm doing a favor for a friend."

"So it's not a job," Maybe said.

"It's a little of both."

"Are you gettin' paid?"

"Uh, no," Clint admitted.

"Then it's a favor."

"What about you? Have you heard anything about would-be stage robbers?" Clint asked. "Anybody looking for that kind of job?"

"There are a lot of men lookin' for jobs," Maybe said, "but so far I haven't heard anythin' about someone wantin' to rob stagecoaches. I'll keep my ear to the ground though. For the next three months anyway."

"Any idea who'll replace you?" Clint asked, as they started walking.

"Seriously? Probably nobody. I think when I retire, so does this badge."

Chapter Nineteen

The next three runs were tense. Clint and Highway Bill were highly aware of their surroundings, their passengers, and the possibilities.

"We should disarm passengers," Bill said, at one point. "They're liable to sneak somebody on board."

"I was thinking about that, too."

But when they approached the ticket clerk, Walker, with the idea he rejected it.

"We don't want passengers made aware that we're afraid we're gonna get robbed," he said. "We want them to ride comfortably."

"That's fine," Clint said to him. "Let's just hope I don't end up having to kill a passenger."

"If you can't tell the difference between a passenger and a robber, you shouldn't be ridin' shotgun," Walker said.

Clint suppressed the urge to smack the man right across the mouth and left the office.

***

After a week had gone by following the shooting, Carl Walker sent a telegram to Denver suggesting the shotgun rider be fired.

"He seems to have done his job," he finished.

But the response wasn't what he had hoped, which was what he told Mary Preston the night before, while they were in bed.

"Can't you get your boss to call him off?" he asked.

"But why?" she said, running her hand over his bare stomach. "Isn't he doing what you wanted him to do?"

"Yes, but now it's over," Walker said.

"Well . . ."

He pushed her hand away and said, "You don't agree?"

"Wait—what?" she stammered as he rose and got dressed.

"I can't be with you if you don't support me, Mary," he said, and stormed out.

The next morning, he was hoping to receive a message from Denver that the shotgun had been let go, but apparently Mary Preston still had not sent her boss that recommendation.

Carl Walker didn't like Highway Bill or Shotgun Sam. He couldn't afford to like them, since there was a good chance they might end up dead. He hadn't yet found men to replace Al Lee and Damian Mair, but when he did, they were going to be made of stronger, tougher stock. And Walker was going to remove one set of instructions from the robberies. No longer would he stress that no one was to be hurt. In fact, he didn't care if Highway Bill was hurt, and he would have been very happy to hear that Shotgun Sam had been killed.

The day went by without hearing from Denver, so that night Carl Walker was in the back room of the Monument Saloon, waiting.

A tall, broad-shouldered man entered the room and stared at him. He was dressed completely in black, which Walker found dramatic.

"You the man hirin'?" he asked.

"That depends," Walker said.

"Your man said I wasn't to tell anybody I was comin' here," the man said, "and I didn't."

The "man" he referred to was the only other man in town who knew what Carl Walker had going. Walker made sure he was never seen anywhere near the office.

"Are you Leo Gordon?" Walker asked.

"That's right."

"Have a seat and a drink. I've got a bottle of whiskey, but I can get you a beer."

"Whiskey's fine," the big man said, and sat. Walker poured him a drink and shoved it across the table.

"Let me tell you what I'm lookin' for . . ."

***

Gordon listened to Walker's explanation, had a few more drinks, didn't ask any questions until the end.

"You want me to kill anybody?"

Walker hesitated, then said, "Just let me say I don't *not* want you to kill anybody."

"So if it comes to it, I can do it," Gordon said.

"Yes," Walker said. "We've got a fella ridin' shotgun who you're going to hafta deal with. I can't get rid of him."

"And you want me to do it," Gordon said.

"Pretty much, yeah," Walker said. "He killed four men who tried to hold up the stage a while back."

"I heard about that," Gordon said. "If I'm gonna hafta deal with this fella, you're gonna hafta pay extra."

"That's not a problem."

"Then tell me about him," Gordon said. "What am I gonna be facin'?"

"I'm not sure," Walker said. "I wasn't impressed when I met him, but when they came back that day with the four bodies on top of the stage, the driver, Highway Bill, was really impressed."

"Did he shoot them all with his shotgun?"

"That's odd," Walker said. "He didn't shoot any of 'em with his shotgun. He used a pistol."

Gordon stared at Walker for a few moments, then said, "I'm gonna hafta get a look at this guy."

Chapter Twenty

There was a run the next morning. Walker arranged to have Gordon in the area so he could get a look at Shotgun Sam.

"Why so empty?" Clint asked, as he entered.

"Only one passenger today, and he's not here yet," Walker said.

"Are we transporting anything else?"

"A lockbox, but there's nothing of value to anyone in it. It's just paperwork. It'll be picked up at the other end."

"And Bill?"

"He's out back, hitching up the team. You better help him. He's getting' fiddle-footed in his old age."

"He's not that old," Clint said, and went out the back.

"'mornin'," Bill said. "Just in time. Gladys is resistin' today."

The team was made up of four mares, and Bill had a name for each of them.

"Here, let me hold her," Clint said, while they got Gladys hitched up with the other three.

"I'll meet you around front," Bill said. "You go on through and get the lockbox."

"Got it."

Clint went back inside, grabbed the lockbox, took it out and tucked it under the seat, since there was nothing else being transported.

"We ready?" Bill asked.

"Not til our passenger gets here."

"He's here," Bill said. "Inside. He was waitin' when I drove around."

"Then let's go," Clint said. "And take your time. I don't think we're in a hurry or in any danger, today."

"That'll be real relaxin'," Bill said, and snapped the reins.

***

After the stage pulled out, the office door opened and Leo Gordon walked in, still dressed in black.

"Did you see 'im?" Walker asked.

"I saw 'im."

"Good," Walker said, "they don't have anythin' of value today, but as soon as we do, I'll let you know. You might want to round up some men while you're waitin'."

"I'll need a lot of men," Gordon said. "This is gonna cost ya."

"Why's that?"

"Do you know who you got ridin' shotgun for ya?" Gordon asked.

Walker paused, then said, "Sam Slade?"

"Huh-uh," Gordon said, shaking his head. "That's Clint Adams."

Walker sat down heavily behind his counter.

"The Gunsmith?"

"That's him."

"You sure?"

"I've seen him more than once," Gordon said.

"Ever go up against him?" Walker asked.

"No."

"Care to?"

"Like I said," Gordon replied. "It's gonna take a lot of money."

"Then we'll save it for a big haul," Walker said. "Get yourself five or six men. Cheap ones you won't mind losing."

"I'll get 'em."

"Tell me where you'll be stayin'," Walker said. "I'll let you know when we're ready."

"The Pine Tree Hotel."

"The other side of town."

"I like it there," Gordon said. "If I'm not at my hotel, I'll be at the Rusty Spike Saloon."

"That *is* the wrong side of town," Walker said. "I don't go over there, just send somebody for me."

"Don't worry," Walker said. "I'll send word."

He turned and left.

"Goddamnit!" Walker shouted.

Langdon Cole just made everything that much harder by bringing in the Gunsmith. And then he realized Mary Preston probably knew and didn't tell him.

He left the office and headed for her hotel.

***

As soon as she opened the door, he backhanded her across the face. She staggered back a few steps, hit the bed with the backs of her thighs and sat on it, her hand to her face.

"What—" she started, but he cut her off.

"The Gunsmith?" he said. "The goddamned Gunsmith, and you couldn't tell me?"

"Wha—how did you find out?" she asked.

"Never mind," he said. "Why didn't you tell me?"

"I—I'd lose my job. Nobody was supposed to know."

"But me?" he said. "Not even me?"

"Mr. Cole and Mr. Adams both agreed—"

"Ah!" he said, waving a hand at her. "Don't bother."

"Why does it matter?" she asked, rubbing her cheek. "Why'd you have to hit me?"

"That's the last physical contact we're gonna have, honey," he said. "We're through. You might as well go back to Denver."

"But . . . are you quitting your job?"

"Not a chance," he said. "I'm just quitting you!"

With that, he slammed the door and stormed off down the hall.

Chapter Twenty-One

"Do we know who this passenger is?" Clint asked Highway Bill.

"Not a clue," Bill said, "but I can tell you he ain't wearin' a gun."

"So this trip's really just for this lockbox," Clint said, tapping the box with the heel of his boot.

"I suppose so."

"A run for a box that doesn't have anything of value in it," Clint said. "How does that sound to you?"

"Like horseshit."

"To me, too," Clint admitted.

"You wanna take a look inside?" Bill asked.

"No," Clint said, "I'm not that curious."

Bill looked disappointed.

"Are you planning on stopping in on Tom and Ginny again?" Clint asked. "Or spending the night in Denver?"

"Denver, I think," Bill said. "I got a little hotel that the stageline pays for. What about you?"

"I've got a place I usually stay," Clint said.

"Any women?" Bill asked.

"Maybe one or two," Clint said, "but not tonight."

"Are you gonna stop and see Mr. Cole?"

"I thought I would," Clint said. "Do you know him?"

"Naw," Bill said, "never met 'im. Wasn't even hired by him."

"Would you want to come with me and meet him?" Clint asked.

"You think it'd do me any good?" Bill asked.

"You never know."

***

They reached Denver and the passenger disembarked without a word to them. He didn't even have a bag up top, just a carpetbag in the back with him.

"I've got to see to the team," Bill said.

"Need my help?"

"Naw," Bill said, "I know the boys here at the station. They'll give me a hand."

"What about going to see Mr. Cole?"

"I don't think I oughtta," Bill said. "I'll just see ya here in the mornin' so we can head back early."

"Okay," Clint said, "see you then."

Clint left the station and headed for the office of Langdon Cole.

***

Cole's girl looked up and smiled at him. Cole had replaced Mary Preston with a girl who was almost her double.

"I know you," she said.

"Clint Adams."

"I saw you when you were here the first time. You look different," she commented.

"It's the clothes," he said. "Is your boss in?"

"Yes," she said, "if you'll wait a moment, I'll let him know you're here, Mr. Adams."

"Thanks."

She got up from her desk and entered her boss's office, reappeared just moments later.

"Go on in," she said.

As Clint entered, Langdon Cole stood up, but didn't come around from behind his desk. He simply stuck his hand out over it for a handshake.

"Happy to see you, Adams," Cole said. "I wanted to be able to thank you for what you did."

"It's only part of the job, Mr. Cole," Clint said. "Roper told me to find out who's behind the robberies, and that's what I intend to do."

"I'm glad to hear that," Cole said. "I must tell you I received a telegram from Miss Preston advising I let you go."

"I think you'll find that suggestion was coming from your ticket clerk, Carl Walker, rather than her."

"What?"

"Miss Preston is, let's say, under his influence."

"Are you saying . . ."

"I'm not saying anything more," Clint said. "If you want to take me off this job, it's fine with me, as long as it's your decision."

"I want you on this job until you find that man or men behind the whole mess," Cole said.

"All right, then," Clint said. "We'll be heading back to Colorado Springs tomorrow."

"We?"

"Me and the driver, Highway Bill."

"Where is he?"

"Taking care of the rig, then going to some hotel he says you pay for when he's in town."

"I'm sure we do," Cole said. "Normally I'd ask Preston about that, but . . . never mind. Do you have accommodations?"

"I do," Clint said. "And when I get in touch with you next, I won't be using the telegraph key that's in the stageline's office."

"Are you saying you don't trust Carl Walker?" Cole asked.

"Let's just say I still want to keep things strictly between you and me."

Chapter Twenty-Two

When they got back to the Colorado Springs station the next day, Clint could feel Carl Walker looking at him differently.

"He knows," he said to Bill, as they unhitched the team.

"Knows what?"

"Who I really am."

"What makes you say that?"

"I can feel it," Clint said, "especially hearing from Cole that Mary Preston suggested he let me go."

"That's Walker's woman, right?"

"Right."

"I guess you gotta watch out for both of them now."

"You might be right about that," Clint said. "What if it's him? What if the ticket clerk is setting up the robberies."

"Of his own stageline?"

"That's just it," Clint said. "It's not his stageline, he just works for it. That gives him all the inside information he needs."

"Then how do you prove it?" Highway Bill asked.

"I have to figure that out."

***

Clint entered Sheriff Maybe's office, found the man sweeping the floor.

"You do broom work too?" he asked.

"Hey, somebody's gotta keep the place clean."

"Why?" Clint asked. "If you're right, it's going to be abandoned in three months."

"I am right."

"What if you're not?"

Maybe leaned on his broom.

"Whataya mean?"

"What if you found the person behind the stage robberies?" Clint asked.

"Why would the people here care about that?"

"Let's say a bank here was sending money to a bank in Denver," Clint said. "Let's say the money arrives safely."

"That would be because of you, not me," Maybe reminded him.

"And if anything happens inside the city limits, Chief Dillon and his men will handle it."

"What if they can't," Clint said, "but you can?"

"Now you're just talkin' in circles, Clint," John C. Maybe said.

"You just be ready when I call on you, John," Clint said.

"And when will that be?"

Clint grinned.

"If I knew that, I wouldn't be talking in circles, would I?"

***

As soon as Highway Bill and "Shotgun Sam" came back to the station, Walker could feel Sam Slade/Clint Adams looking at him differently. If Adams suspected him, he was going to have to be very careful. The tension was why he was startled when the telegraph key began chattering. He ran over to read the message. It was a single line, and he didn't like it: MEET TONIGHT.

Only one person would send him a message like that, and this would be the first time he met with this person face-to-face. All other instructions had come via the telegraph key. This had to have something to do with the way Adams was looking at him. He knew he would have to be convincing that there was no problem.

***

Walker arrived at the Monument Saloon first and seated himself at the table in the back room. He preferred sitting there when it was he who called the meeting. But the way it stood now, he was very uncomfortable.

It was a lively night at the Monument, with the noise level very high. He sat with a gun in his lap, just in case, and felt fairly sure he'd be able to fire off one shot without attracting attention. If it came to that, of course.

He was very surprised when the curtain parted, and Mary Preston walked in.

"What the hell—" he started, but he was surprised again when she produced a derringer and shot him in the chest. He tried to lift his own gun but couldn't.

She came around the table and plucked the gun from his hand, then stuck both her gun and his into her purse, which was large enough to carry both.

"Just so you know," she said to him, "this has nothing to do with the smack in the face you gave me. This has to do with you wearing out your welcome, Carl. Now I need to find somebody else to do the job."

She turned and walked out.

Chapter Twenty-Three

When the knock came on the door of Clint's room, he grabbed his gun, got out of bed and padded barefoot and bare-chested to it.

"Who is it?"

"Chief Dillon."

Clint opened the door a crack, looked at the chief, and opened it wider. The man was standing in the hall alone.

"What brings you here this early, Chief?" Clint asked.

"Murder, I'm afraid. May I come in?"

"Sure."

Clint walked to the bedpost, holstered his gun, then grabbed his shirt and put it on.

"Who got murdered," he asked, "and why does it involve me?"

"Fella named Carl Walker. You know him?"

"You know I do," Clint said. "He's the ticket clerk at the stage station. What happened?"

"He was shot last night," Dillon said. "Once in the chest."

"Where'd it happen?"

"The back room of the Monument Saloon," Dillon said. "They actually found him this morning when they came down to clean the place up. Looks like he'd been sitting there all night. You ever been to the Monument?"

"No," Clint said, "can't say I have. I've been to the one downstairs and the Starlight."

"Can I see your gun?"

"Sure."

Clint withdrew the gun from the holster again, sprang the barrel, unloaded it and handed it to the chief.

"You're a careful man," Dillon said. "I could shoot you with my own gun, you know."

"I know," Clint said. "I just don't ever want to be killed with my own gun."

The chief sniffed the barrel and handed it back.

"Hasn't been fired," he said.

"Not lately," Clint said, holstering it. "Not since the attempted robbery."

"Doesn't smell recently cleaned either," the chief commented.

"Oh, it's been cleaned, but you're right, not recently," Clint said.

"It looks like Walker was shot with a small caliber gun, maybe even a derringer. You own a derringer?"

"No. I have another gun, but it's a thirty-two caliber. Do you want to smell that one?"

"No need," Dillon said. "I didn't really think you did it. You got any idea who might?"

"Well," Clint said, "I guess I can tell you now I was starting to suspect that he had something to do with the robberies."

"Like what?"

"Supplying inside information," Clint said, "or even planning them himself."

"So you think somebody involved with the robberies killed him?" Dillon asked. "A falling out among thieves?"

"Could be."

"Who else in town is involved with the stageline?"

"There's a woman named Mary Preston here at the hotel. She works for the company."

"I suppose I should speak to her then. What room is she in?"

Clint told him Mary's room number.

"You should know something else about her," Clint said.

"What's that?"

"She's been sleeping with Walker."

Dillon's eyebrows went up.

"You think there was a lover's quarrel?"

"Who knows?" Clint said. "She doesn't strike me as the type to shoot her lover, but you never know, do you?"

"Not when it comes to love," Dillon said.

"You mind me asking why you're looking into this yourself?" Clint asked.

"My department doesn't have a detective yet," Dillon said.

"Why don't you promote somebody?"

"I don't have anyone qualified," Dillon said. "Say, how would you like—"

"No thanks," Clint said, "my days of wearing a badge are way in the past."

Dillon shrugged and said, "It was just a thought." He walked to the door, put his hand on the knob, then turned back. "Who will be running the stage office now?"

"Your guess is as good as mine," Clint replied. "Like I said, Mary's the only employee here in town, so I guess she'll have to step up."

"I don't suppose she would've killed him for his job," Dillon commented.

"I think she likes the job she has in Denver, Chief," Clint said.

"And why wouldn't she?" Dillon said. "All right Mr. Adams. Sorry if I woke you."

"Time for breakfast anyway," Clint said.

"For you, maybe," Dillon said, and left.

Chapter Twenty-Four

Clint had breakfast alone in the hotel dining room, thinking about the murder of the ticket agent. If it had nothing to do with the robberies, it probably wasn't going to change anything. If it did have something to do with the robberies, it might keep him riding shotgun for a lot longer than he had planned.

He entertained the idea of going to Mary's room to see how she was taking the news, but in the end decided to simply go to the station. When he got there, Highway Bill was standing outside with his arms crossed, as if waiting for . . . something.

"You heard?" he asked, as Clint approached.

"I did," Clint said. "The chief knocked on my door early this morning."

"He's in there now, with Mary Preston," Bill said. "I think they're sending a telegram to the home office in Denver."

"Makes sense," Clint said. "Somebody's going to have to make a decision."

"You ready to take over?" Bill asked.

"Not me," Clint said. "I told the chief Mary was the only employee in town, but I forgot about you."

"I'm just a driver," Bill said. "I ain't runnin' nothin'."

At that moment the door opened, and the chief stepped out.

"Looks like she's been put in charge, for now," he said. He looked at Bill. "How did you get along with Carl Walker?"

"Just fine," Bill said. "He did his job, and I did mine."

"Well, I'll head back to my office, send some men to look at Walker's room."

"I wish you luck," Clint said.

"You'll let me know if it turns out this has something to do with the robberies, right?"

"You'll be the first one I tell," Clint lied.

As the chief walked away, Clint said, "I guess we better go inside and see if we have a run today."

"I'm right behind ya," Bill said.

As they entered, they saw Mary standing behind the desk, somewhat disheveled, but dry-eyed. Clint noticed a bruise on her cheek. A lover's quarrel? He wondered.

"Mary," he said, "I'm so sorry to hear what happened."

"So am I," she said. "I've been in touch with Denver and Mr. Cole has told me to take over, until I can hire a replacement."

"He wants you to do the hiring?"

"Yes."

"Do we have a run today?"

"Not today," she said. "I think we have to shut down at least one day in honor of Carl, don't you?"

"Well . . . sure."

She looked past Clint.

"Bill, we'll make a run tomorrow morning."

"Yes, Ma'am. I'll be here."

"You can take the rest of today off."

"Thank you, Ma'am," Bill said. To Clint he said, "See ya."

As he left the office, Mary said to Clint, "Lock the door, will you?"

"Sure."

He did so and turned to face her.

"Do you know who killed Carl?" she asked.

"No, I don't."

"Any idea why he was killed?"

"It might have had something to do with the robberies. Or maybe with that bruise on your cheek?"

Her hand flew to her face.

"This? No, we just . . . got rough one night."

"Ah."

"You think Carl was involved with the robberies?"

"Could be," Clint said. "Involved, or actually planning them."

"He was a handsome man," she said, "and a good ticket agent, but I don't think he was that smart."

"You'd know that better than I would," Clint said.

"Mr. Cole wants you to stay on the job," she said.

He didn't bother telling her that he and Cole had already had a conversation.

"No problem there," Clint said. "I haven't done what I came here to do."

"Unless you suspected Carl of planning these robberies and killed him for it."

"First of all, I would've had to do more than just suspect him," Clint said. "And even if I knew he did it, I wouldn't kill him. I'd have him arrested."

Her shoulders slumped and she said, "I'm sorry, I just—I mean, your reputation—"

"Never mind," he said. "I know you're upset. I'm sure you have some work to do, being in charge and all, so I'll see you in the morning for tomorrow's run."

"Clint? Would you have supper with me tonight at our hotel? I just need to talk."

"Of course. What time?"

"Seven?"

"I'll meet you in the dining room at seven," he said, and left.

Chapter Twenty-Five

As soon as Clint entered the sheriff's office, John C. Maybe held his hand up.

"I heard," he said. "Have a seat. Want some coffee?"

"Why not?" Clint said, as he sat.

Maybe went to the potbellied stove in the corner, poured two cups and handed one to Clint.

"I thought I might see you over at the station," Clint said.

"What for? Wasn't Chief Dillon there?"

"He was."

"Well, there you go," Maybe said. "He wouldn't have wanted to see me."

"You know, it's too bad Walker got killed, but this could be a good opportunity for you to show this town who's more valuable, you or Dillon. He admits he has no detective in his command."

"I'm no detective either, Clint," Maybe said.

"Sort of puts you on equal footing, doesn't it?" Clint asked.

"Or," Maybe said, "it puts me ahead, if I've got you on my side."

"That's right."

"Got any idea about who killed the clerk?"

"Not yet," Clint said. "I told Dillon he'd be the first to hear when I did, but I'd rather tell you. That is, if you'll do something about it."

"You get me somethin' to work with," Maybe said, "and I'll do somethin'."

"Deal," Clint said.

***

Clint had never been to the Monument Saloon. It was a large place, offering everything a man could want. But early in the day, it was cavernous and almost empty. He approached the bar and the unsmiling bartender.

"A little early," the man said, "but we have what you want."

"I want to talk."

"That'll cost, you," the man said.

"Why don't we see if you really do have what I want before I pay?"

The bartender was big and beefy, in his fifties and gone a bit to fat. But Clint still wouldn't have wanted to tangle with him.

"What's on your mind?" the man asked.

"You know a man named Carl Walker?"

The bartender frowned.

"Why you askin'?"

"Because he got killed in your back room last night."

"That don't mean I knew 'im."

"But you found him this morning, right?"

"One of my girls did," the bartender said.

"Had you ever seen him in here before?"

The bartender apparently decided to stop deflecting and just tell the truth.

"From time to time."

"To drink in the back room?"

"Every so often he'd wanna meet somebody in private," the man said. "I let him use the room."

"Because you were friends?"

"Because he paid me."

"Do you own this place?" Clint asked.

"I just work here and pick up an extra dollar now and then."

"I see." That probably meant he ran the girls, too, but Clint didn't care about that.

"Was he here last night meeting somebody?"

"Yeah, he paid me like always, then went in the back to wait."

"And you didn't notice that he never left?"

"Mister, if you came here at night, you'd see how hard it is to keep an eye on one person."

"Yeah, I bet this place is jumping when it's busy."

"Every night."

"Has the law been here yet?"

"That Chief of Police?" the bartender said. "Oh, yeah."

"What'd you tell him?"

"Nothin'."

"What about the girls? Did he talk to them?"

"No."

"You mind if I do?" Clint asked. "Maybe one of them saw something."

The bartender folded his arms and stared. He stayed that way until Clint put a few dollars on the bar.

"Go on upstairs," he said. "You can knock and see if they answer."

"Each girl have her own room?"

"Yeah."

"How many girls?"

"Five," the bartender said. "When you come back down from talkin' to them, you're gonna want a beer. I'll have it waitin'."

"I appreciate that."

He left the bar and went up the stairs.

Chapter Twenty-Six

Four girls were groggy when they opened the door, answered him shortly, flirted out of habit, and then slammed their door shut.

The fifth girl had been awake for a while and allowed him to enter. Clint was surprised she was a beautiful Chinese.

"Don't be so surprised," she told him. "There's no Chinatown here, so I'm an attraction. You mind if I brush my hair while we talk?"

"Not at all."

Her hair was a beautiful curtain of black that went halfway down her back. Her English was perfect. She sat at her dressing table, started running a brush through her hair, and regarded him in the mirror. She wore a long robe with red and yellow dragons on it.

"Why are you so much more alert than the other girls?" Clint asked.

"I wake up earlier than they do," she said. "To brush my hair."

"What's your name?"

"Ying."

"Why is your English so good?"

"I came to this country as a small child," she said. "I made sure, as I got older, my English got better." She raised her eyebrows at him in the mirror. "Not that I didn't occasionally say 'so solly' or 'no tickee, no shirtee' when the time is right."

"Ying, did you know the man who was killed here last night?"

"I didn't know his name," Ying said, "but I've seen him here before."

"In that back room?"

"Yes."

"Have you ever seen who he met with?"

She started brushing her hair and turned to face him.

"One time."

"Last night?"

"No, but a couple of nights ago he met with a big man, dressed all in black. That was why I noticed him. He stood out even as he walked across the crowded saloon."

"A big man dressed in black."

"Yes, wearing a gun on his right hip. The holster was also black."

"Black leather holster," Clint said, frowning. It jogged something in his memory.

"You mean a black suit, like a gambler?"

"No," she said, "just a black shirt, a black vest, pants, boots . . . everything."

She brought her hair down over her shoulder so she could brush it while facing him.

"What's this to you?"

"I work for the stageline. He was the ticket clerk."

"What was he doing having meetings here?" she asked.

"That's what I'm trying to find out."

"Sorry I can't help more," she said.

"That's okay," he said. "You've told me some things I didn't know."

He headed for the door.

"Hey," she said.

He turned and looked.

"Come back some night when I'm looking better."

"You look pretty damn good right now," he said, and left.

She turned to look in the mirror. She knew he would be back and was determined to look better than damn good.

***

As promised, the bartender had a beer on the bar waiting for him when he came down.

"That was a lot of talkin'," the man said. "Builds up a thirst."

"It sure does. Thanks." Clint drank half of it down. "Have you seen a big man dressed in black around here?"

"Dressed in black?" the bartender said. "I'd notice that."

"With a black leather holster."

The bartender rubbed his jaw.

"You know, I think I saw somebody like that a coupla nights ago."

"Here, at the bar?"

"No," the bartender said, "just walkin' across the floor."

"Toward the back room?"

"Maybe."

"Did you see him last night?" Clint asked. "Think about it."

"No," the barman said, "no, not last night. You think that's who killed 'im?"

"He doesn't sound like a man who'd use a derringer, does he?" Clint said.

"Come to think of it, no he don't."

Clint finished his drink and set the glass down.

"Thanks for the cold beer."

"The girls any help?"

Clint decided to lump Ying in with the others.

"They were all pretty mad I woke them," he said, "and not real helpful."

"Too bad," the bartender said. "Come back tonight when they're workin'. They'll be in a better mood."

"Maybe I'll do that," Clint said. "Thanks."

Chapter Twenty-Seven

Clint arrived at the hotel dining room and found Mary Preston already seated at a table.

"Thanks for coming," she said.

"No problem." He sat opposite her. "You said you wanted to talk."

"Yes," she started, but the waiter came over and they ordered first. Then Clint just waited for her to speak again. "You know that Carl and I were . . ."

"Yes."

"But that doesn't matter now," she said. "He's dead, and the business has to go on."

"I agree."

"I'm going to interview some men for the job, but I anticipate doing it myself for a while."

"Is that what Mr. Cole wants?" Clint asked.

"It is."

"I'm with you, then," he said.

"You mean Shotgun Sam is with me?"

"That's right," Clint said. "I have to stay Shotgun Sam for a while longer."

She smiled and said, "Let's eat."

***

After supper, they walked out to the lobby together.

"Would you . . . like to come up to my room?" she asked.

"I don't think so," he said. "It wouldn't be a good idea. After all, I work for you now, don't I?"

"Yes, I suppose you're right," she said. "Good night."

As she crossed the lobby and went up the stairs, Clint left the hotel and headed for the Monument Saloon.

The bartender had been right about the place. It was packed with customers drinking, gambling, and grabbing at the girls. The bleary-eyed stares were gone, replaced with beautifully made up faces—especially Ying. Her hair was lustrous, her gown jade green and yellow, and her lips were blood red.

"Came to have a look, huh?" the bartender said to him.

"That's right. I'll have a beer."

The bartender drew him a cold one and set it down without spilling a drop.

"Care for a little gamblin'?" he asked. "Maybe a girl?"

"I'm not gamblin' these days," Clint said, "and I don't pay for girls."

"Enjoy your beer, then."

"Have you seen that fella in black tonight?"

"Nope, no sign of 'im. But, hey, he could be in here and I didn't see him. Take a walk around."

"I think I will." Clint picked up the beer.

"On the house," the barman said.

"Thanks."

Clint took his beer and started walking around the floor. The girls recognized him as the man who had awakened them that morning and chose to stay away. All but Ying. When she saw him, she smiled and walked over.

"Welcome," she said.

"You look stunning," he said.

"Really?" she asked. "That's not a word I hear in here very often. Thank you."

"I'm looking for that man in black," Clint said. "Have you seen him in here today?"

"No, I haven't," she said. "I'm disappointed."

"Why?"

"I thought you came here to see me."

"Believe me, Ying," he said, "under other circumstances . . ."

"So in other words, another time?"

"Exactly."

"Then I have to go back to work," she said. "I'll see you."

She turned and melted into the crowd. Clint set his beer down on a nearby table and left.

***

Mary Preston sat on the bed and considered her options. She'd had no choice but to kill Carl Walker. She enjoyed letting him take her to bed and have his way with her. She allowed him to think he was in charge. But he was losing control of the situation, and so he had to go.

Now she had to find someone else to act for her. Just as Clint felt he had to remain Shotgun Sam, she felt she had to remain the girl who worked for Langdon Cole. That meant she needed the right man to replace Walker.

She knew Walker had a man he used to find him his crew. She was going to have to trust that same man to find somebody for her. And the only way to trust him was going to be paying him too well for him to do anything other than what she wanted. She didn't know what Carl Walker had been paying, but with Carl's death fresh on everyone's mind, she was going to have to pay him more.

But first she was going to have to find him.

Chapter Twenty-Eight

When Clint arrived at the station the next morning, Mary Preston was all business.

"Bill's out back," she told him. "You're going to have three passengers today."

"A lockbox?"

"No," she said. "I don't think you'll have to worry about robbers today, but I know you'll be alert anyway."

"Yes, I will."

He went outside to help Bill finish hitching the team and then loading the coach as the passengers arrived. Three men, each with a carpetbag.

"We ready?" Bill asked.

Clint climbed up and sat beside him.

"Ready."

Clint looked at the office, saw Mary watching them through the window. Behind her a man was sweeping the floor. He'd seen him in there once or twice before.

"Let's roll," he said.

***

After the coach pulled away, Mary went behind the desk to take care of some paperwork.

"The floor's clean, Miss," the man with the broom said.

"Good, thank you."

"Anythin' else I can do for you?"

"The stable out back probably needs some cleaning out," Mary said.

"I'll take care of it," he said. "Anythin' else you need?"

She looked up from the desk at his face. He was in his forties, kind of short and ugly, but he was smiling at her.

"What's your name?" she asked.

"Me? I'm Oscar."

"Who hired you, Oscar?"

"That'd be Mr. Walker," Oscar said. "I'm sorry about what happened to him."

"Oscar, what did you do for Mr. Walker?" Mary asked.

"Sweep, clean," Oscar said, "and a little of this and that when he needed somethin' extra."

"And when you did these things, did he pay you extra?" she asked.

"Oh yeah."

"Oscar," she said, "do you think you could do some extra things for me? That is, if I pay you?"

"Whatever you want, Ma'am."

"Well, I'm looking for a man . . ."

***

Leo Gordon was smart enough to stay away from the Monument Saloon after hearing that Carl Walker had been killed. However, there were other, smaller saloons that men like him frequented in different parts of Colorado Springs, and Oscar knew where those saloons were.

"Been lookin' for you," he said, approaching Gordon, who was sitting alone at a table with a beer in the Renegade Saloon.

"That right?"

"Can I sit?"

"What's on your mind, Oscar?"

"The stagecoach."

Gordon frowned.

"You thinkin' I killed that fella?"

"No, that ain't it a-tall," Oscar said.

"Then sit." As the smaller man took a seat, Gordon waved at the bartender for two beers.

"Thanks," Oscar said, and drank some. "Look, I don't know what you and Walker had goin' on, but now there's a woman where he used to be, and she wants to hire somebody."

"To do what?" Gordon asked.

"I don't know," Oscar said. "All I'm bein' paid to do is connect the two of you."

"She asked for me?"

"No," Oscar admitted, "she just said she needed somebody, and I know you do . . . what would you call them . . . odd jobs?"

"Some odder than others, but that's fair," Gordon said. "When and where does she want to meet?"

"Well," Oscar said, "not at the Monument Saloon, that's for sure."

"I don't blame her for that."

"How about here?" Oscar asked.

They both looked around at the dull finish on everything in the place, including the people.

"She's a lady," Gordon said. "Would she come here?"

"I guess if you guarantee her safety," Oscar said.

"If there's a payin' job bein' offered, I can do that," Gordon said.

"What should I tell her about the law?" Oscar asked. "They're gonna be pokin' around about the killin'."

"You know," Gordon said, "this town thinks it has a spankin' brand new police department, but all they really have is confusion. Tell her not to worry about the law."

"Okay," Oscar said. He finished his beer and set the empty mug down. "Tomorrow night?"

Gordon nodded.

"Midnight," he said, "the Renegade is deader than usual, then."

"Midnight it is," Oscar said, and left.

Chapter Twenty-Nine

At midnight, Mary Preston walked into the Renegade Saloon. She'd decided to disguise herself in a shirt and hat that were too big for her, hiding her true shape and gender. Luckily, there was only one person in the saloon other than the bartender, and it was the one she was looking for.

She walked to the back table where Leo Gordon was sitting.

"Gordon?"

"That's right."

"Oscar told me I'd find you here."

"Siddown," Gordon ordered.

She sat across from him.

"You want a drink?" he asked.

"No."

"Talk, then."

"I've got a job I need done," she said. "Do you have any problem with holding up stagecoaches?"

"Am I gettin' paid?"

"Yes."

"Then no," he said, "I don't have a problem with that. Lay it out for me . . .

***

After she finished, Gordon said, "I've got some questions."

"Go ahead."

"Were you workin' with Carl Walker?"

"No," she said, "he was working for *me*."

"Did he know he was workin' for you?"

"No," she said, "we never did business face-to-face. And I left it to him to get the men he needed."

"But you were givin' him inside information."

"He was the ticket clerk who ran the station here," she said. "He was getting his own inside information."

"Why?"

"Why what?"

"Why were you doin' this?" Gordon asked. "Why *are* you doin' this?"

"I'm going to tell you something I haven't told anyone else, so you'll understand. My father was one of the owners of the stageline, until Langdon Cole forced him out. It broke him and he killed himself. This is my way of getting justice for him," she said. "Now, do you want the job or not?"

"If you want me to go up against the Gunsmith, you're gonna have to pay real well."

"I'm ready to do that."

"When's the next stage you want hit?"

"I'll let you know that," she said. "First, I want Adams and the driver to get complacent. Maybe they'll think the robberies are finished. That's when you'll hit. Meanwhile, you'll have time to get your men together."

"Don't worry about that," he said. "I know just who I'm gonna use."

"Good," she said. "I'll use Oscar again the next time I want to meet. Is this place good?"

"It's fine," Gordon said. "Nobody's gonna give a damn if we meet here."

"Then you'll be hearing from me," she said, and headed for the door.

"Hey!" Gordon called.

"Yeah?" she asked, turning back.

"What's your name?"

"Mary," she said, and left.

After she was gone, the bartender came over to Gordon's table and put down a fresh beer.

"What was that about?"

"Business."

"What kind of business?"

Gordon looked up at him.

"My business," Gordon said. "Bring me a bottle of whiskey. That's your business."

"Right."

***

Mary got back to her hotel room, removed the hat and shirt. Standing there naked to the waist, she thought about the big man in the saloon. He interested her, but that would have to come later. If it worked out that he was able to do the job with the robberies, then maybe she'd give him something else to do. But for now, she'd have to do it for herself.

She removed her boots and trousers, then reclined naked on the bed. Using one hand to pinch the nipples and rub her hard little breasts, she slid the other hand down between her legs and began to rub. But instead of thinking about Leo Gordon, the man in black, she thought about Clint Adams, the man down the hall . . .

***

Clint considered going down the hall to Mary Preston's room, but decided it would be better to keep his distance. After all, when this was all over, he was going to have to make sure she paid for her crimes. That would be easier to do if he did not become involved with her on a very personal level . . .

Chapter Thirty

Clint became bored with his room, his book, and with thinking about the stage robberies. He decided to go to the Monument Saloon and give it a real close look while it was in full swing. And then maybe he'd stop by the Starlight Saloon and have a beer with John C. Maybe, if he was around.

However, since he passed by the Starlight first, he decided to go in. As large and busy as the Monument, he managed to elbow himself some room at the bar and get Mike's attention.

"Beer," he said.

"Comin' up."

"Seen the sheriff?" he asked, as Mike served him his beer.

"Earlier," Mike said. "He'll probably be back in."

Clint picked up his beer and looked around. His eyes found each of the three girls working the floor. They were pretty enough, but not as interesting looking as Ying.

Clint turned, put his half-finished beer down on the bar.

"If you see him, tell him I was here," Clint said. "If I can get back, I will."

"Sure thing."

Clint started to leave, then turned back.

"Mike, what do you know about the Monument Saloon?" he asked.

"Good place," Mike said. "Second best in Colorado Springs."

Clint didn't have to ask which saloon Mike thought was the best in town.

***

Clint entered the Monument, realized that although it was similar in size to the Starlight, it was noisier. He wondered if that was because the Starlight had a higher ceiling with the window there.

He went to the bar and elbowed in, excusing himself when he caused one man to spill some beer.

"Sorry about that," he said.

"Don't worry about it," the man said, and turned back to the bar.

"Beer," Clint said.

The fat bartender gave him a beer.

"I haven't seen your man tonight. You here to talk to the girls again?" he asked.

"Maybe." Clint sipped his beer. "Actually, I'm just looking for something to do. I was getting bored in my hotel room."

"In that case," the bartender said, "enjoy yourself. There's plenty to do here."

"I can see that."

The bartender moved on down the bar. Clint turned with his beer in hand, scanned the room and everything that was going on around him. As he watched, Ying once again appeared and approached him.

"You look lonely," she said.

"Do I?"

"Yes. Would you like to come to my room for a while and talk?"

"Is that an invitation?" he asked. "Or an offer of business?"

She smiled.

"It's an invitation," she said. "I am not a whore."

"I'm sorry—"

"No need to apologize," she said. "Some of the girls do sell sex for extra money. I don't."

"Then I'd be happy to come to your room and . . . talk," he said.

She smiled.

"Follow me."

She led him across the crowded floor, and a path seemed to open ahead of her. They went up the stairs to her room. She closed the door and turned to face him.

"Would you like a drink? I keep some whiskey here," she offered.

"Yes, that'd be good."

"Then sit."

He looked around. The only places to sit were at her dressing table or on the bed. He sat at the foot of the bed. She took a whiskey bottle from a dresser drawer and two glasses. She poured about two fingers of amber liquid into both glasses, handed him one, then sat on the chair by her dressing table, facing him.

"Whatever it is you're doing here in Colorado Springs," she said, "are you growing tired of it?"

"Oh, yes."

"Then why don't you leave?"

"I'm afraid I'm committed to finishing what I started," he told her.

"I see," she said. "And you're a man who always fulfills his commitments?"

"Yes."

"I guess that's not always a good thing," she said, "is it?"

He sighed, said, "Apparently not," and drank his whiskey.

Chapter Thirty-One

"Is talk what you really wanted to do with me?" she asked.

"I think you know the answer to that."

She smiled knowingly, put her glass down on the dressing table and stood up. Reaching behind her, she undid her gown and allowed it to flutter to the floor. She wore nothing underneath, not wanting to obstruct the view for the men downstairs, showing just enough to tease for tips.

But here in this room, with Clint, she smiled as she showed it all.

She was a short woman, about five-two, with smooth, silky looking skin, small breasts with dark brown nipples, and a wild tangle of black hair between her thighs. Her long black hair was a shiny curtain on her shoulders. He could feel the heat emanating from her body across the room.

And then she came closer.

"Let me help you undress," she said, reaching for the buttons on his shirt.

He placed his hands on her hips as she peeled his shirt off, her skin hot on his palms. Then he slid his hands up her bare back and pulled her to him so he could kiss her breasts and nipples.

"Wait, wait . . ." she said pushing away from him, "you still have too many clothes on."

She reached for his gunbelt, but he put his hand on hers.

"I can't get your pants off with that around your waist," she pointed out.

"It has to be close by," he said.

"All right," she said, "but I promise you won't need it with me."

He unstrapped his gunbelt and took it off, handed it to her, watched her hang it on the bedpost, which was exactly where he would've put it.

"All right?" she asked.

"Fine."

She came back, then, got to her knees in front of him. She helped him off with his boots and trousers, then sat back on her haunches and stared at his hard penis as it jutted out at her.

"Oh my," she said, simply, and reached for him. As her hands closed over his hard cock, he realized this was what he needed to relax him. Tomorrow, he'd be able to think much more clearly about things.

Tonight, there was no thinking required, at all . . .

***

After satisfying her needs herself, Mary Preston donned a nightgown and got under the covers of her bed. She was happy with her meeting with Leo Gordon and had the feeling that this man was going to be able to get the job done. Carl Walker had been useful—in more ways than one—but in the long run, she never really thought he was the man for the job. With the appearance of Clint Adams on the scene—unexpected, to say the least—it seemed she had been right. She needed a man more equipped to do the job on the trail. As far as a new clerk for the office went, she would take her time hiring one.

She knew her boss, Langford Cole, had big plans for the Colorado Springs/Denver stage and had been hoping all her pieces would be in play by the time the plans came to fruition. The death of Walker might have changed her plans, but now that she had seen Leo Gordon, she was back to thinking everything would be in place when the time came.

All she had to do was convince Cole he could go ahead with his ultimate plans.

***

Clint put his arms around Ying as she slid into his lap, trapping his penis between their bodies. She rubbed the hair of her crotch over him as she kissed him, and as her pussy began to grow moist, she wet the length of him. Finally, she lifted her hips and came down on him, taking him fully inside her hot vagina.

"Oh," he said.

"I know," she moaned, letting her head drop back. "You fill me perfectly."

"You're hot," he said. "Like an oven."

"Have you ever been with a Chinese girl before?" she asked him.

"Yes," he said, "but it's been a while."

"That's good," she said, moving on him, rocking herself back and forth, then up and down. She put her hands around his neck and pulled his face to her breasts. He took her nipples in his mouth, rolled them, bit them hard enough to make her squeal and move faster on him.

Clint wrapped his arms around her and bore her down onto the mattress with him, so they were no longer seated. She got comfortable sitting atop him, pressed her hands down on his sternum for balance and began riding him up and down so quick and hard the sound of their flesh slapping together filled the room . . .

Chapter Thirty-Two

Later, after she rode him until she experienced every ounce of pleasure it would bring, she got down between his legs and took him into her sweet mouth. He filled his hands with her lovely hair, held her lightly as she bobbed up and down on him. She kept at it until he couldn't hold out anymore and simply exploded into that mouth . . .

***

"Did that fix your problem?" she asked later, as they lay together in her bed.

"It helped," he said, "a little."

She slid her hand up onto his chest and twisted one of his nipples.

"Ow! Okay, okay, it helped a lot."

She released him, slid her hand down to his belly, where she made circles.

"Do you want to tell me what your problems are?" she asked.

"No," he said, "it's better if you don't know."

"Can you stay all night?" she asked.

"I'm afraid not." He swung his legs out and planted his feet on the floor. He grabbed his pants and pulled them on. She set her almond-shaped eyes on him as he dressed and strapped on his gun.

"Will you come back?" she asked. "The next time you're feeling lonely?"

"Is that an open invitation?" he asked.

"It is."

"Then yes," he said. "I'll be back."

"Tell the bartender to give you what you want on the house. Tell him I said so."

"He'd do that on your say so?" he asked.

"Of course."

"Why?"

She smiled broadly.

"He works for me," she said. "I own the joint."

***

He had his free beer at the bar, still shocked by her revelation. He was impressed that a Chinese girl, so young, could own a place like the Monument Saloon.

"She told you, didn't she?" the bartender asked.

"What's that?"

"That she's the boss."

"Oh yeah," Clint said, "that. Yes, she told me."

143

"She likes to keep it to herself," the man said. "She must like you a lot if she told you."

"What's your name?" Clint asked. "Nobody's told me that, yet."

"My name's McCullough, but everybody calls me Mac."

"Well, thanks for the beer, Mac," Clint said. "I'll see you around."

"I bet you will," Mac said and winked.

Clint turned and left the still bustling saloon.

***

Over breakfast the next morning, Clint figured that, for now, his only move was the move he was already making. Ride shotgun on the runs, wait for the stage to be hit again. When it happened, he would have to do his best to keep at least one stage robber alive. At the moment, his only suspect in town, somebody with enough knowledge of the stage schedules to set up the robberies, was Mary Preston, herself. That might have seemed impossible to him, if he hadn't met and spent time with Ying and found out that the young Chinese girl owned the second best saloon in town.

After that, anything was possible.

***

After breakfast, he walked to the stage office. As usual, Highway Bill was hitching up the team, and passengers were waiting in the office, seated on benches. Mary Preston was behind her counter.

"'mornin'," she greeted him.

"Good-morning . . . Ma'am," Clint said, in his best Shotgun Sam Slade voice. There were four passengers—three men and a woman—and two of them looked up at Clint and Mary as they greeted each other.

"Lockbox today?" Clint asked.

"We've got one, but there's nothing special in it. I already gave it to Bill."

"Okay, then."

As Clint started for the back, Mary said, "I think he can manage the team. Why don't you get the passengers outside and ready to board?"

"You're the boss, Ma'am," he said, changing direction. He stopped in front of the seated passengers. "Okay, folks, let's get outside and you can tell me what bags are yours."

Chapter Thirty-Three

Once they started driving, Clint asked Highway Bill, "How well do you know Mary Preston?"

"Not that well."

"When did you meet her?"

"When I first got this job," Bill said, "a while back."

"Was it Cole who hired you?"

"I was supposed to see Langdon Cole and apply for the job, but when I got there, it was Mary I ended up talkin' with."

"Wait, Mary Preston hired you?"

"Yes."

"What about the other driver, O'Shea?"

"Yeah, he told me once she was the one who hired him," Bill replied.

"So what the hell does Cole do?"

Bill shrugged.

"Whatever a general manager is supposed to do," he said. "I guess he's the one who hired Mary."

"That makes sense."

They rode in silence for a while, and then Highway Bill said, "How long do you think she's gonna be our new ticket clerk?"

"I don't know," Clint said. "Maybe until she hires somebody else for the job."

"Don't look at me," Bill said. "I tol' you before, I'm a driver."

***

Once both stages were gone—the Trinidad run, and Denver run—Mary Preston left the office and locked it behind her. Oscar hadn't come in to clean the office that day. He usually did it every other day. On the off days, she knew he cleaned other locations, mostly saloons. She wanted to find him, but that would take too long. There were over twenty saloons in Colorado Springs.

As it turned out, the only other way was to wait until he showed up the next morning . . .

***

Clint and Bill made the run to Denver and back without incident. They spent the night in Denver again. On the trip back, the stage was empty. There was no chance of a robbery, as they were carrying nothing. They rode most of the way in silence, alone with their own thoughts.

***

Mary Preston waited impatiently for Oscar to arrive the next morning with his broom.

"'mornin'," he said, as he walked in.

"Forget the broom, Oscar," she said. "I need you for something else."

Oscar cackled and said, "I know that ain't like it sounded."

"Please . . ." she said.

"Yeah, yeah, I know," he said. "You're lookin' for somebody."

"That's right."

"Who?"

She told him . . .

***

Clint and Highway Bill rode into Colorado Springs in the late afternoon. The office door was open. Bill drove the coach right around to the rear, and they both dropped down to the ground.

"Need help?" Clint asked.

"I've unhitched a hundred teams," Bill said. "You do what you gotta do."

"I'll see you later, then," Clint said.

"I'll stop by the Starlight for a beer."

Clint needed to get some sleep, but that wasn't what he was going to do. He left the stable feeling worn out and went into the office by the back door, expecting to find Mary Preston there, but it was empty. A check of the front door showed that she had locked it. He decided to have a look around and see if there was anything that would be helpful to him.

He went behind the ticket counter and searched every nook and drawer, finding nothing. It was too much to hope that she had left a tell-tale telegram behind.

A further search of the office revealed nothing. Neither Carl Walker nor Mary Preston had left anything damning behind when they departed.

In the end, he let himself out the back door and started walking toward his hotel.

***

Mary and Oscar walked through town and stopped at a saloon on the wrong side of the tracks called The Buffalo Chip Saloon.

"You shouldn't be in places like this," Oscar told her, as they entered.

"I'm not the delicate little flower you think I am," she assured him.

They got a beer each and sat at a table together ignoring the looks from other customers.

"What's on your mind, then?" Oscar asked.

"I need you to give Leo Gordon a message for me," she said.

"Is he workin' for you?"

"He is."

"That's all I do," Oscar said. "I put people together. I don't deliver messages."

"Then work for me," she said. "I'll pay you to be the go-between for me and Mr. Gordon."

"What about cleaning your office?"

"I'll hire somebody else to do that," she said. "All I want you to do is be where I can find you when I need to send him a message."

Oscar sipped his beer. Mary took some money from her purse and slid it across the table to him.

"That's for a start," she said.

He looked down at the paper money on the table, then looked at her and asked, "What's the message?"

Chapter Thirty-Four

Mary Preston's message to Leo Gordon was delivered that night by Oscar in the Rusty Spike Saloon.

"She wants me to do what?"

"Kill the Gunsmith here in town," Oscar said. "She don't want you to wait and do it on the trail during a robbery."

"Why not?"

"Because during a robbery it might not get done," Oscar said. "And because on the stage he'll be expectin' it."

"She doesn't think a man like Clint Adams expects to be killed every day?"

"She expects that you'll get enough men to get it done," Oscar said.

"Then you tell 'er it's gonna cost 'er," Gordon said.

"She knows that."

"And not just money."

"Whataya mean?"

"I mean that little lady's got some fire in 'er," Gordon said. "I wanna feel it."

"Are you sayin'—"

"You know what I'm sayin'," Gordon said. "You just tell 'er that."

"I'll tell 'er," Oscar said, "but I don't know what she's gonna say."

Gordon smiled.

"I do."

***

"Tell him yes," Mary said.

"You know what he wants, right?" Oscar asked. "He wants you to—"

"Yes, I know what he wants," she said. "But I need what I want, too. So . . . tell him yes. Find out where and when. Agree to anything."

"Are you sure about this?"

They were in the office, and Mary had just discovered that it had been searched. It didn't take her long to decide by who. Something had to be done about Clint before the next robbery was planned and carried out, because it was probably going to be the big one.

"I'm sure, Oscar."

He stared at her a moment longer, then said, "I guess you were tellin' me the truth."

"About what?" she asked.

"You're not the delicate flower I thought you was."

***

Leo Gordon was right where Oscar had left him, only with a fresh beer.

"She says yes," he told the big man. "You name the when and the where."

"Well," Gordon said, rubbing his big jaw, "she don't wanna be seen together, and she don't mind comin' over to this end of town, so I guess a hotel . . . I'll pick one and let you know."

"She must have somethin' real important to her for you to do, if she'll agree to this," Oscar said.

"I guess I'll be findin' that out," Gordon said, then with a wide grin he added, "after."

***

Mary Preston locked the door of her hotel room and sat on the bed. She wished she could convince Clint Adams to work with her, but she knew him well enough now to know he would never agree to it. He was too honest, and too damned honorable.

This was not the time of her life when she wanted to meet a man like that.

Chapter Thirty-Five

Over the next three days they made two more runs. Clint still had not met Paddy O'Shea, the driver who made the Trinidad run.

"You don't want to," Bill said, when Clint mentioned it on the third morning.

"Why not?"

"He's not a pleasant guy," Bill said. "He's never had anybody ride shotgun with him in all the years he's been drivin'."

"Because he never gets robbed?"

"Because nobody wants to ride with 'im," Bill said.

"He's that unpleasant?"

"Unpleasant, and smells bad"

"Then how does he keep his job?"

"Easy," Bill said. "He's good at it. I ain't never seen nobody get so much out of a team than he does."

"He's better than you?" Clint asked. "I find that hard to believe."

"Okay, maybe he's the second best."

"Have I ever seen him around town?" Clint asked. "In a saloon, maybe."

"You'd know by the smell if you had."

"So where does he eat and drink?"

"Wherever the least amount of people go," Highway Bill said. "Nobody likes to eat or drink around him—except for a couple of friends who smell the same way."

"There are more?"

As they got the coach ready to go—carrying two passengers but no lockbox—Bill said, "Do you wanna meet 'im? Is that why you're askin'?"

"I was just wondering if he'd know anything about what's been going on," Clint said.

"I can't say," Bill replied, "but if you wanna talk to him, I guess I could hunt 'im up for you when we get back."

"Good," Clint said, "Let's do that tomorrow."

"As long as we can spend the night at Tom and Ginny's station tonight and not Denver."

"Agreed."

***

"During the day?" Mary said to Oscar, that same morning. The former sweeper came in after Highway Bill and Clint left on their run.

"That's what he said," Oscar told her. "Seems he can't get a room at night without payin' for it."

Mary rolled her eyes and looked around the office.

"All right, I'm not needed here, right now," she said. "When does he want me?"

"In an hour," Oscar said.

"Where?"

"A hotel called The Dark Rose."

"Really?"

Oscar shrugged.

Mary sighed.

"Okay, tell me where it is . . ."

***

Mary walked into the lobby of the Dark Rose Hotel and could smell the dust. She walked to the front desk where a desk clerk in last week's suit stared at her. His shirt cuffs and collar were frayed.

"Can I help ya, lady?" he asked.

"Leo Gordon?"

A nasty smile came over the man's face.

"Room one-oh-seven," he said. "Have a good time."

She ignored him and went up the stairs. When she knocked, Gordon answered quickly.

"Come in," he invited.

She stepped into the room carefully, in case there were other men there, as well, but there weren't.

"Oscar told you what I want?" Gordon asked. "Just to be clear."

"He said you want to fuck me," she said, "and then you'll work for me."

"Wow," Gordon said, "he was clear, wasn't he."

"Let's get this over with, Mr. Gordon," she said. "I have things to do and, when we're done here, so will you."

They started to undress, and Mary was not at all distressed by the sheer mass of the man.

"I've got to ask," she said, folding her clothing. "Why would you want this—me—instead of more money?"

"Oh, I'm gonna ask for more money," Gordon told her, "but you're a pretty little woman and I like the idea that I'm gettin' paid to poke you, and not the other way around, like with a whore."

"I see." She turned to face him, totally nude. His cock was engorged and veiny, she was very curious about how it was going to feel. "Let's get this done," she said.

Chapter Thirty-Six

Gordon was almost hypnotized by the feel of Mary Preston's soft, smooth, pale flesh.

Mary found herself entranced by the man's huge cock.

So they spent more time together than either of them had planned. Gordon had just wanted to lay with her one time, and then move onto business.

Mary wanted to give the man what he wanted, one time, so that he would give her what she wanted.

It didn't work out that way . . .

***

"My God," Mary said, hours later. "That thing is almost lethal." She reached over and stroked the man's cock which, while relaxed, was still larger than any she had ever seen.

"And your quim whiskers," he said, moving his hand down between her thighs, "is amazin'."

"Okay, wait," she said, slapping his hand away from her cunt and scooting away from him. "We need to discuss business before we start anything, again."

"Really?" he asked, finding his cock himself so that it started to harden.

"Leo!" she scolded. It was during the time when he was fucking her from behind, putting her on her hands and knees, that she began to shout out his name, "Leo! Leo!"

"Oh, all right." He moved his hand and pulled the sheet over his crotch. "Talk. What got you involved in this stagecoach business, anyway?"

"It's complicated," she said, "but my plan is to drive the stageline into bankruptcy. I told you before, I want to see Langdon Cole on his knees in the street."

"And that's gonna happen by robbing the same stage over and over again?"

"Within the next week," she said, "the stage is going to be carrying a lockbox with more money in it than ever. Most of that money *belongs* to the stageline. We take it, and they're done."

"And that ticket clerk, Walker, was helping you?"

"He thought he was," she said. "I just used him for a while."

"And is that what you're gonna do with me?" Gordon asked. "Use me?"

"Probably," she said, "but for a lot longer than I used him, believe me."

"So," Gordon said, "you need me to first kill the Gunsmith, and then rob the stage."

"Exactly."

"And why don't we just kill him while we're robbin' the stage?" Gordon asked. "After all, he's actin' like a shotgun, right?"

"Right, but wouldn't that be too risky?" she asked.

"Not with the men I'm gonna recruit," he told her. "They're all experienced and they'll all jump at a chance at Clint Adams. Also, killin' him here in town means we'd have to deal with the law. Killin' him out on the trail will make that harder. The law will take a while to decide who should deal with it."

Mary decided not to push to have Clint Adams killed in Colorado Springs. Her discussions with Leo Gordon now had her convinced that the man knew what he was doing—out of bed, anyway.

It was not his prowess in bed that had her fascinated, but his physical presence. Over the course of time she thought she would be able to show him what she wanted in bed. But first things first, getting rid of Clint Adams and destroying the stageline and Langdon Cole.

There was a sudden quick knocking on the door at that point.

"Who's that?" she snapped.

"Relax," Gordon said, "It's just a signal that we have to leave the room."

They both got out of bed, took a long, last look at each other, and then began to get dressed.

"You go first," he said. "I'll find a place for us to meet next time where we won't be bothered."

"I'll send you a message with Oscar when we're ready for the big pay day."

"I'll be ready," Gordon promised.

She patted his chest and said, "So will I."

***

Mary went back to the stage office and let herself in, locking the door behind her. Then she sent a telegram to Langdon Cole, telling him that it was time for the transfer of money from Colorado Springs to the stageline offices in Denver. Cole was figuring on using the money to expand operations. Mary was planning to steal the money, so that the stageline would be forced to close up shop and go out of business. And Langdon Cole would be out of a job, the way he had forced her father out years before.

It was time for revenge.

Chapter Thirty-Seven

The next afternoon Highway Bill and Clint returned from their run. When Clint entered the office, the telegraph key was chattering, and Mary was bent over it.

"Something important?" he asked.

She turned quickly and stared at him, a look of almost panic on her face. But when she saw it was him, she relaxed.

"Clint! You startled me. Did you just get back?"

"Yes," he said, "Bill's unhitching the team."

"Good, good," she said. "I think I'll have a run for you tomorrow, but I'll let you know for sure."

"Okay," he said. "I just wanted to tell you we were back. I'll go and help Bill."

"You do that."

He started for the back door, then turned and pointed at the key.

"That thing was chattering away when I came in," he said. "Funny it's quiet now."

"It wasn't anything real important," she told him. "They're just waiting for my reply."

"I won't keep you, then," he said, and went out the back.

***

"What's goin' on?" Bill asked.

"I don't know," Clint said. "Something."

"What makes you say that?"

"The telegraph key was jumping when I went in, and Mary looked like she got caught doing something she didn't want anybody to see."

"Maybe you just surprised her," Bill offered, still bent over the stage.

"Could be."

Bill stood and looked at Clint.

"You thinkin' maybe that girl's behind the robberies?"

"Maybe somebody's threatening her, making her cooperate," Clint said. "They may have killed the ticket clerk, figuring that would get her moved into the job."

"Well," Bill said, "if that was what they wanted, they got it, but it ain't permanent-like, is it?"

"Probably not," Clint said, "but they may not have wanted it to be permanent. Just for now might work for them."

"Then you're thinkin' we're gonna get robbed again, and soon," Bill said.

"Could be."

"So what are we gonna do?"

"We're going to be ready for them," Clint said.

***

Clint took Bill to the Starlight Saloon for a drink. While they were seated, he was surprised to see Sheriff John C. Maybe walk in. It was early for the sheriff to be in the saloon. The lawman spotted them, got himself a beer from the bar, and walked over.

"Mind if I join you?" he asked.

"Have a seat," Clint said. "We were just going over our options."

"Oh yeah?" Maybe said, sitting. "What'd you come up with?"

"It's what Clint comes up with," Bill said. "Me, I'm just drivin."

"So?" Maybe asked. "Whataya got?"

"We wait."

Maybe stared at him, and then said, "That's it?"

"That's it."

"Wait for what?"

"The reason this has all been happening."

"And what do you figure that is?"

"I think the reason the same stage has been getting robbed might be that they were practice jobs."

"Practice?"

"Rehearsals," Clint said. "For the real thing."

"What makes you say that?" Maybe asked.

"Somebody's been planning these robberies," Clint said. "Why? The take has been paltry, at best. And according to Bill, each time the robberies were pulled by a different man, or men. I think it's all aiming at something bigger."

"Any idea when?" Maybe asked.

"I'd say soon," Clint said. "All we have to do—Bill and me—is keep making our runs until the big one."

"Big one?" Maybe said.

"The day there's something valuable in that lockbox."

"That could take forever," Maybe said. "Are you willin' to wait that long?"

"I'm committed to seeing this through," Clint said. "And I don't think it's going to take as long as you might think."

"And what are you basin' this one on?" the lawman asked.

"Let's just say I have a feeling," Clint said. "An instinct."

"And you're willin' to depend on this instinct?"

"My instincts don't usually let me down," Clint said. "I can't imagine whoever's been planning these little jobs is going to be satisfied with them. No, there's something bigger coming."

Chapter Thirty-Eight

Mary Preston looked up from her desk as the office door opened and Clint Adams walked in.

"Clint," she said. "I was just getting ready to close up. I didn't think I'd see you again until tomorrow's run."

"I've had some thoughts about these robberies and wanted to bounce them off you."

"Sure," she said, "go ahead."

"I think they're leading up to something big."

"Oh? Like what?"

"I was hoping you'd tell me," Clint said. "Have you had any word from Cole in Denver about something big coming up?"

"No," she said, "just the usual passengers and lock-box. You know, now that you bring it up, I've always wondered why they keep hitting this stage when there's never a lot of money on it. I'd think they'd hit it coming from Denver, or from Denver to Gunnison—you know, figuring a bigger amount of money would be coming *out of* Denver."

"That's an interesting point," Clint said. "Look, if you hear anything from Cole about a big shipment, you'll let me know, right?"

"Of course," she said. "After all, you're riding shot-gun."

"Yeah, right," he said. "I am."

"Are you still using Shotgun Slade as a name?"

"For now," he said.

"Okay, then," she said. "I'll see you in the morning . . . unless you want . . . something else?"

"No," he said, "nothing else. See you in the morning."

Clint left the office, thinking he needed to contact one other person.

***

"Whataya got?" Highway Bill asked when Clint arrived the next morning. He was earlier than usual, stopping in the back while Bill was hitching up the team.

"It's the telegram," Clint said, "from Denver. I sent one to Langdon Cole, and he answered me right away."

"What's it about?" Bill asked.

"He's planning to send a large amount of money to Denver on this stage soon."

"When?"

"He was going to do it days ago, but the robberies changed his mind. That's why he wanted to hire my friend Roper, and how I came to be here. He wants the robberies stopped so he can ship the money."

"What'dya tell 'im?" Bill asked.

"I told him to go ahead and ship it."

"Why'd you tell 'im that, if you're waitin' for another robbery?"

"I'll explain . . ."

***

Clint and Bill walked the coach around from the back so they could start loading it. There were four passengers waiting on the bench inside the office.

"Did you explain it all to Cole?" Bill asked.

"No, there's too much to put in a telegram," Clint said. "When we get to Denver I'll stop in and see him."

"You wanna push and get there tonight?"

"No," Clint said, "let's just go easy, make our stops at the stations, and spend the night at one of them. I can talk to him tomorrow."

"Okay," Bill said, "whatever you say . . . Sam."

"Let's get these passengers loaded," Clint said. "I'll go in and get them."

"Suits me," Bill said.

***

They spent the night at one of the stage stopovers, changed teams one more time at Tom and Ginny's stop before arriving in Denver.

"What now?" Bill asked, after turning the coach and team over to the Denver crew.

"Let's go and talk with Cole," Clint said.

"You want me to go with you?"

"Yes."

Bill shrugged and said, "Why not? I got nothin' else to do."

"Then let's go."

***

They got in to see Cole after Clint convinced his new girl he was Clint Adams and not actually a reprobate named Sam Slade.

"Sorry about that," Cole said. "Mary has been impossible to replace. I've got to bring her back from Colorado Springs soon."

"I think she might be getting pretty comfortable there," Clint said.

"Well, she's given me the go ahead to make my big shipment," Cole said. "And now that you have—"

"Yeah, about that," Clint said. "We have to talk."

Chapter Thirty-Nine

"Are we safe here?" Mary asked Leo Gordon.

"We can have this room for as long as we want," he told her.

She looked around at the drab furnishings, the dust and, most of all, the grimy sheets.

"Um, yeah," she said, "I don't think I can stay that long, Leo. I've got plans to make."

"Then why'd you tell Oscar you wanted to see me?" the big man asked. "I thought you want—"

"That's going to have to wait," she said, cutting him off. "I got a telegram this afternoon."

"Who from?"

"My boss, in Denver," she said. "He said he's going to be sending the money on the next stage."

"Next? When is that?"

"Two days," she said. "Can you get your people together by then?"

"No problem," he said.

"Good," she said. "Then do it."

"Where do you want us to hit the stage?" he asked.

"I'm working that out," she said. "I'll let you know tomorrow."

"And can we spend some time together then?" he asked, looking hungry.

She looked around at the awful room again, but then thought about his big, thick, veiny cock and said, "I'll work something out."

**

Clint and Bill got back from Denver that evening, after Bill pushed the team they got at the last stopover.

"These poor bastards," Bill said, unhitching them.

"They've got all day tomorrow to recover."

"Naw," Bill said, "we'll just leave here with another team. These four can make the Trinidad run. There's no hurry with that one."

"Suit yourself," Clint said. "You're the driver."

As Clint started away, Bill asked, "Where are you off to?"

"A steak," Clint said, "with Sheriff John C. Maybe."

"You gonna make him part of this?"

"Oh yeah . . ."

**

Clint found the lawman at the Tenderloin Steakhouse.

"Mind if I join you, John C.?"

"Mr. Adams," John C. Maybe said. "Have a seat. I only just ordered."

Maybe got the waiter's attention and held up two fingers. The waiter nodded his understanding.

"You just get back?" Sheriff Maybe asked.

"Yeah, I was in Denver, talking with Langdon Cole."

"How did that go?"

"We came to an understanding."

"What kind of understanding?" Maybe asked.

"Let's wait for our steaks," Clint said, "and I'll tell you while we eat."

***

After steaks and beer, coffee and pie John Maybe looked across the table at Clint and asked, "So this is how you wanna play it?"

"If you'll go along with it," Clint said. "I'm guessing after I took care of those four, there's going to be more, next time."

"That's probably true," Maybe said, "but why don't you ask Chief Dillon for some men?"

"Because I'm sure he'll say it's going to happen outside his jurisdiction."

"You're probably right about that," Maybe said.

"I know you're looking forward to your retirement—" Clint started.

"Oh, shut up about that," Maybe said.

"Then you're willing?" Clint asked.

"I'm willing. When will it be?"

"Day after tomorrow," Clint said. "Come to the stage office early, but not out front."

"Gotcha," Maybe said, standing. "I got rounds to make now. Starlight later?"

"I'll be there," Clint said, "and the drinks will be on me."

***

Clint went from the steakhouse to his hotel, decided to clean his guns before heading for the Starlight Saloon. With any luck, his days as "Shotgun Sam Slade" were coming to an end. If that was the case, he was going to make sure that the shotgun and his Colt were clean and ready to be used.

***

Leo Gordon knew he was working for Mary Preston, but he had second thoughts about the way she wanted to handle the Gunsmith. Gordon didn't know how many people actually knew that Adams was acting as the stage shotgun. What the hell was the difference if some unknown shotgunner got himself shot in the back? And he knew plenty of fellas who felt that when it came to somebody like the Gunsmith, shooting him in the back was akin to a fair fight.

Chapter Forty

When Clint got to the Starlight Saloon, Sheriff John C. Maybe was already there. As he started for the bar, Ying came out of a crowd of men who were trying to get her attention and walked toward him.

"It has been a while," she said.

"I know," he said. "I've been real busy."

"As long as you were not dissatisfied with me the last time," she said.

"Not at all," he said. "I'll definitely be coming to see you again."

"Then I will let you go," she said. "I can see your friend is waiting for you."

And she melted back into the crowd.

When Clint got to the bar, Maybe already had a beer waiting for him.

"That little lady seems pretty friendly when it comes to you," the lawman said.

"We've spent some time together."

"Ah . . ."

They both turned their backs to the room and leaned on the bar. Clint was careful to keep an eye on the mirror, though.

"Given any more thought to your problem?" Maybe asked.

"A bit," Clint said, "but I haven't changed my mind."

"I didn't think you would."

"I just need to take at least one man alive," Clint said. "I need somebody to point out the ringleader."

"But you've got an idea who it is, don't you?"

"I'm afraid I do," Clint said.

"Well," Maybe said, "if things go your way, you won't be Shotgun Sam for very much longer."

"That'll suit me," Clint said. "It's not a job I think I could do every day. There's just too much back-and-forth for me."

"You think that's monotonous, try bein' a lawman," John C. Maybe said. "Pretty much the same, day in and day out."

"Oh, I know that," Clint said. "I had my years behind a badge in my younger days. Got pretty tired of them quick."

"You've probably done a little bit of everythin', ain'tcha?" Maybe asked.

"Pretty much," Clint said, "and it all gets monotonous after a while."

"Life's that way," Maybe said, "and retirement ain't gonna be no different."

"You just have to keep finding reasons to get up in the morning," Clint told him.

"Well," Maybe said, "not bein' retired would be one reason."

"There you go," Clint said. "We solve these bank robberies and put the ringleader away, and maybe you won't be voted out."

"Or forced out," Maybe said.

In the mirror Clint could see Ying standing with some men who were talking to her, but she was looking over at him. There really was no reason not to spend some more time with her. He turned and looked at her, and she got the message and came walking over.

"Looks like you figured out a way to break the monotony," the lawman said.

"Why not? We've got nothing to do tomorrow," Clint said. "Just remember to meet me at the stage office the morning after."

"I'll be there," John C. Maybe said. "You just make sure you got the energy to be there, too."

As Ying approached, he put his empty mug down on the bar.

"Don't you worry," he said to John C. Maybe, and stepped forward to meet Ying.

"You change your mind?" she asked.

"I did."

"Good." She took his hand and led him across the room to the stairs, followed by the envious stares of every other man in the room.

***

There were three men in the saloon who were watching as Clint and Ying walked across the room, but they weren't watching the Chinese girl. They were watching the man they had been told was called Shotgun Sam Slade.

"Whatawe do now?" one man asked. "He's goin' upstairs with that Chinese gal."

"We wait for him to come back down," another man said. "What else can we do?"

"We been told to kill 'im," the third man said. "We could go upstairs and catch him with his pants down."

"We could," the first man said, "but then we'd probably have to kill that gal, too."

"That'd be a shame," the second man said. "She's pretty popular."

"Yeah," the third man said, "we'd probably never get out of the saloon alive if we did that. We better wait."

They ordered three more beers.

Chapter Forty-One

Ying was out of her dress quickly, and just as quickly her dark-tipped breasts were in Clint's hands. He usually preferred larger breasts, but there was something about the Chinese girl's body that was perfect. The curtain of long black hair added to the effect.

Once again the gunbelt went on the bedpost, and then Ying peeled his clothes off. When she had him naked, she knelt in front of him, ran her hands up the back of his legs to his buttocks, which she gripped while rubbing her cheeks and mouth over his hard cock. When he was fully erect, she opened her mouth and took him inside, as deeply as she could, and then began to suck him avidly, while digging her nails into the tender flesh of his buttocks.

She suckled him to the point of exploding, then released him and shoved him back onto the bed. As she crawled on top of him, intending to impale herself on him, he grabbed her and flipped her over so she was on her back.

"Not yet," he said. "It's my turn."

"Your turn?"

He spread her thighs and got down between them.

"Really?" she asked, with a smile. "No man's ever done that to me before. I'm always the one—"

"Well, this is pleasure, not business, Ying," he said. "This time it's all for you."

He bent to his task . . .

***

Leo Gordon entered the Starlight and found his three men sharing a bottle of whiskey.

"What the hell is goin' on?" he demanded, sitting with them.

"We're waitin'," one said.

"For what?"

"Shotgun Sam," another man said. "He's upstairs with the Chink girl."

The third man said, "I wanna go up there and do it, but these two don't wanna kill that Chin-ee girl."

"She's too pretty," the first man said.

"And everybody here would kill us," the second man said.

"Good point," Gordon said, grabbing the whiskey bottle. He took one drink and stood up. "Get 'im when he leaves."

"Right," they said.

"And let me know when it's done."

He got up and walked out.

"Let him know when it's done," one of the men said. "Where's he gonna be?"

"I know where," the first man said. "That flea bag of a hotel." He got up.

"Where ya goin'?"

"To get another bottle of whiskey."

***

Ying had her hands on the back of Clint's head as he avidly licked up her juices. She just kept getting wetter and wetter, as if it would never stop, and then abruptly she wrapped her fingers in his hair and yanked his face away from her.

"Enough!" she croaked. "Oh my God, enough!"

He got up onto his knees, still between her thighs, and looked at her.

"Enough pleasure?" he asked.

"I would never have thought pleasure could kill me," she said, staring at him, her almond eyes moist, "but if I let you keep doing that, I think I will die—I'd die happy, but I'd die!"

He laughed.

"I guess it's a good thing I don't have men doing that to me every night," she said.

"Are you sure?" he said, reaching his hand out to her.

Abruptly, she drew her knees up to her chest and wrapped her arms around them.

"Wait, wait," she said, "I need a minute."

He sat back, his cock still hard and jutting up at her.

"Where did you learn to do that to a woman?" she asked.

"Just over the years," he said.

"Most men just rut and sleep," she said. "They couldn't care less about a woman's pleasure."

"Those are the kind of men who need whores," Clint said.

"I can see why you never pay for a woman," Ying said. "You don't have to."

She stretched her legs out then, and reached up with her arms, took a deep breath.

"Okay," she said, "I'm ready."

He stretched out next to her, so that their bodies were touching. Then he took her in his arms and kissed her. Her hand slipped down between his legs and began stroking him. He allowed one hand to glide down her back to her buttocks, slid one finger along the cleft between her perfect buttocks.

They kissed that way a long while, their legs entwined, and before long he found her moist vagina and slid easily into her . . .

Chapter Forty-Two

When he came down a few hours later, he was once again subjected to the envious stares of the men remaining in the saloon. The customers with jobs were gone, since they had to be at work the next day. The ones remaining had nothing better to do and would probably stay forever if the saloon never closed.

Clint stopped at the bar for one more beer.

"I can't remember the last time a man stayed up there with Ying for that long," the bartender said. "You must have a lot of money."

"No," Clint said, "I don't." He drank the beer down, said "Thanks," and headed for the door.

***

"Finally!" one of the men said as Clint came down.

"That Chinese whore musta made a lot of money," one of the others said.

"Maybe he's got some left," the third man said. "We'll check his pockets after we kill 'im."

He started to rise, but the first man put his hand on his arm, stopping him.

"What—

"Let him get outside," the first man said, "and start for his hotel. We've got time."

They waited a few more moments, then all three stood up and walked to the door.

***

The streets were quiet, which was why it wasn't hard for Clint to hear three men coming up behind him. In the glow of one of the street lamps, he suddenly turned, and the men froze in their track.

"What was the plan?" he asked. "Shoot me in the back?"

"We don't know what you're talkin' about," one of them said.

"Look, I saw you in the saloon when I went upstairs, and I saw you when I came down," Clint said. "Now here you are on my heels. It's no coincidence."

Two of the men looked very nervous. The man in the center was a little calmer, but not by much. Somebody was going to go for their gun.

"Let's just take it easy," Clint said.

"We can take 'im," the middle man said. "It's three against one, and there's nobody else around."

"Now hold on," Clint said, "I just want to talk—"

The middle man went for his gun. The other two were a split second behind him. That made them multi-seconds slower than Clint, who only needed a split second to beat them to the draw. People sometimes asked him why he had to kill people. Why not just shoot to wound them in the hand, or the leg? But since he had no advance notion of how good they were, and things were happening quickly, he had no time for trick shooting. A wasted second could mean life or death.

But he did want to keep one of them alive to question. So when he drew, he shot the men on each end in the chest. The man in the center, the spokesman, he assumed had the leadership role of the three. He shot that man in the right shoulder, which caused him to immediately drop his gun from his right hand.

"What the hell—you didn't use your shotgun," the man said.

The shotgun hung uselessly from Clint's left hand. It was only part of his Shotgun Sam persona.

"Stand still," Clint said, "while I check your friends."

The man clutched at his shoulder and squeezed his eyes shut.

"Geez, this hurts!"

"You should've thought of that before you decided to shoot me in the back," Clint said, bending over the other two. "They're dead."

At that point, men came running over to see what the disturbance was—and one of them was Sheriff John C. Maybe.

"Ah," he said, "now I see," as a crowd began to gather.

"These three intended to shoot me in the back, Sheriff," Clint said. "As you can see, I killed two. This one is going to tell us who put him up to it."

"I need a doctor," the man said. "I'm bleedin' to death."

"The rest of you men, get these bodies over to the undertaker."

"He's closed," somebody said. "And asleep."

"Then wake him up!" Maybe shouted. He looked at Clint. "We better get this jasper to the doc. We'll have to wake him up, too."

"Let's go . . . what's your name?" Clint asked the man.

"I'm bleedin' . . . he said, again.

"We can get his name later," Maybe said. "Let's see about keepin' him alive, first."

At that point the man collapsed, so Clint and Maybe were forced to carry him to the doctor's office.

Chapter Forty-Three

"He's dead," the doc said.

"Whataya mean, he's dead?" Sheriff Maybe demanded, "He was only shot in the shoulder."

"The bullet hit an artery," the doctor said, drying his hands on a towel. "I couldn't stop the bleedin'."

"I guess I should've shot him in the knee," Clint said, shaking his head.

"It doesn't matter where you shoot a man," the grey-haired sawbones said. "The shock to his system could kill him. If he was gonna die, he was gonna die."

"Did he say anything?" Clint asked.

"He whimpered a lot," the doctor said. "Sorry. Sheriff, could you get some men to take him to the undertaker?"

"I'll take care of it, Doc."

The old sawbones said, "Thanks."

Clint and Maybe stepped outside.

"Goddamnit!" Clint said.

"Don't blame yourself, Clint," Maybe said. "You heard the doc. It didn't matter where you shot him, he coulda died. You're just gonna have to stick to your plan."

"Losing these three men might put things off," Clint said.

"What makes you so sure these three were connected with the robberies?" Maybe asked. "Could be they just recognized you and decided to try takin' you."

"That's a good point," Clint agreed. "Okay, so back to the original plan."

"Which means you'll have to stay alive all day to-morrow," Maybe said. "Stayin' in your room might be smart."

"Hiding has never been my strong point," Clint said. "As long as the word doesn't get all over town about who I really am, I should be all right."

"Why don't I walk with you to your hotel, just to make sure you get there," Maybe said. "Then tomorrow we can have breakfast—"

"What do you intend to do, babysit me all day tomorrow?" Clint asked.

"Why don't we just start with breakfast?" Maybe suggested.

"Okay," Clint said, "but we can include Highway Bill. I want him to be in on everything."

"And Miss Preston?"

"You and Bill are the only people in town I trust," Clint said.

"Okay," John C. Maybe said, "breakfast for three, it is. And I know just the place."

***

Clint managed to get to Bill the night before, so they met in the lobby of the hotel, where they waited together for John C. Maybe to arrive.

"You know," Bill said, "I ain't got nothin' against lawmen, but I gotta say I ain't never had breakfast with one."

"He's going to help us end these robberies, Bill," Clint said.

At that moment, Sheriff Maybe entered the lobby.

"Ready?" he asked.

"The steakhouse?" Clint asked.

"No," Maybe said, "I know another place that serves a great breakfast. Gents, follow me."

Maybe turned and went back out the door.

"What if he's leadin' us into a trap?" Bill asked Clint.

"I've decided I trust two people, Bill," Clint said. "You, and him."

"You trust me?" the stage driver asked.

"Probably even more than I trust him," Clint said. "Let's go. I'm hungry."

***

When Leo Gordon didn't hear from his men the night before, he knew something had gone wrong. By morning he heard the news, and knew he was going to need more men.

And he knew just where to get them.

***

Mary Preston heard the news the next morning that three men had tried to kill "Shotgun Sam Slade." She just hoped it was the work of three idiots, and that Leo Gordon hadn't gone off and made a decision on his own.

She'd be getting together that night with Gordon to make sure the plan went off without a hitch the next day. After that, she had decided to take the money and get as far away from Denver as she could—maybe New Orleans. Nobody would ever find her there, and she would be able to live the life she wanted to live.

***

At breakfast, Highway Bill listened as Clint went over his plan.

"Are you sure this is gonna happen tomorrow?" Bill asked.

"I can't be sure of anything, Bill," Clint said, "but along with Langdon Cole's cooperation, we've got it set-up to happen tomorrow. Whether it does or not will be up to the stage robbers."

"Are we gonna have any passengers?"

"I don't know that either," Clint said. "I guess that'll depend on whether or not Mary sold any tickets. If Cole was smart, he will have told her to leave the coach empty."

"Passengers could get in the way," Maybe said.

"You're right," Clint said. "If there are any, we may have to dump them soon after we leave town."

"They won't be happy about that," Highway Bill said.

"But they'll stay alive," Clint said. "We don't need any innocent bystanders catching a stray bullet."

"So you don't think we can get out of this without any shots bein' fired, huh?" Bill asked.

"I doubt it," Clint said, "but one way or another, I'm keeping at least one of those crooks alive—even if I just have to shoot off a toe."

Bill looked at Maybe.

"A toe?"

"That's a story for later," Sheriff Maybe told the driver.

Chapter Forty-Four

The next day went by without anyone trying to kill Clint. He didn't need Sheriff Maybe to babysit him, but he stayed in his room, worked on his weapons yet again, including his shotgun.

Highway Bill and John Maybe went their own way, and the three of them met in the stable behind the stage office the following morning.

"What now?" Bill asked.

"You hitch up the team," Clint said. "I'll go inside, see if we have any passengers, and get the lockbox. I'll meet you out front."

"Right."

Clint looked at Maybe.

"You know what to do?"

"I do."

Clint nodded, headed into the stage office.

***

Mary Preston spent the night with Leo Gordon, who claimed he didn't have anything to do with the three men who tried to kill Clint Adams.

"They must've recognized him and made the mistake of bracin' him," Gordon lied.

Mary wasn't sure if he was lying or not. It was likely, but he was prepared to do what had to be done the next day. And she was prepared to do what had to be done after that.

Four guards from the Bank of Colorado Springs, as well as the vice-president, arrived at the office that morning soon after she did, and the shipment was put in the lockbox.

"I can leave the guards here," the vice-president said.

"No," she said, "that would just raise suspicion that something very valuable is in the box. You all just better go. We'll handle it from here."

She was alone with the lockbox when Clint Adams entered the office. He no longer looked like Shotgun Sam, but that didn't matter.

"What've we got?" he asked. "Any passengers?"

"No," she said, "today it's just the box." She pointed. "I'll get it."

"You're going to need help," Mary said.

"Why?" Clint leaned down to lift the box but found that he couldn't.

"Gold?" he asked, straightening.

"Mr. Cole and the bank thought gold would be harder to steal than cash," Mary said. "Especially if the robbers were expecting cash."

"Yeah, they'd be really disappointed when they tried to lift this," Clint said, "but resourceful men would find a way."

"That's why you're here, isn't it . . . Shotgun?" she asked. "You and Bill better get that box stowed."

"Wouldn't it be better—and safer—just to put this on a buckboard and drive it to Denver?"

"Mr. Cole wants it delivered by one of our coaches," Mary told him. "And he's the boss."

"Right," Clint said, "he's the boss."

He went outside to get Bill.

***

Once they had the box on the coach and stowed away, Clint and Bill got in their seats. Clint leaned down.

"What're you doin'?" Bill asked.

"This trip," Clint said, "it's the shotgun that rides under the seat."

"Right," Bill said, and snapped the reins.

Chapter Forty-Five

"Are we gonna need that?" one of the men asked Leo Gordon, pointing at the buckboard.

"We are," Gordon said.

"It's just that, it's kinda hard to outrun a posse in a buckboard," the man said.

"Ain't gonna be no posse," Gordon told him, "so don't worry about that."

He looked at the eight men he had gathered for this job, all sitting their horses anxiously because they had been told it was a big job. What they had not been told was that the man riding shotgun on the stage was Clint Adams, the Gunsmith. Gordon didn't think they needed to know that. He had made the mistake of telling three men, and he was sure their nerves had gotten them killed.

"We're gonna do what we have to do to take this stage," he told them. "The lockbox we want is going to be heavy, so we're gonna need time to load it onto our buckboard. You know what that means."

"We gotta kill everybody on that stage," one man said.

"If that's what it takes," Gordon said, "then that's what we'll do."

"When and where are we doin' this?" somebody asked.

"They're leaving Colorado Springs right about now," Gordon said. "As soon as they're out of the town limits, we hit them. We'll be out of the law's jurisdiction."

"So nobody's gonna come after us?" someone asked.

"If they try," Gordon said, "it'll be after we're long gone. Now, everybody check your weapons, and we'll get goin'."

***

"When do you think they'll hit?" Bill asked Clint as they drove out of Colorado Springs.

"Probably when we get outside of everyone's jurisdiction," Clint suggested. "They know there's confusion about who the law is, because of this new police department. It would take quite a while before a posse took off after them."

"If somebody got back to town alive to tell the tale of what happened," Bill added.

"Yeah, there is that."

"You know," Bill said, "if you ain't gonna use that shotgun, you mind if I use it?"

"Be my guest," Clint said.

"I don't mind tellin' ya, I'm nervous as hell," Bill said. "I wouldn't hit a thing with my rifle."

Clint reached under the seat, brought out the shotgun and said, "It's all yours."

Bill took it and set it down next to him, where he'd be able to get at it quickly.

"Okay," he said, "let 'em come."

***

"There it is," Gordon said.

He had split his men, four on one side of the road, and three with him on the other side. One more man was lagging behind with the buckboard.

"How do you know?" one man asked.

"I can hear it," Gordon said. "It's gonna come around this bend, and when it does, we're gonna hit it from both sides."

"Are they gonna be expectin' us?" another man asked.

"It don't matter," Gordon said. "Just make sure you all fire at the shotgunner. He's the only one we got to worry about."

"Do you know who he is?" another man asked.

"Yeah, I do," Gordon said. "He's the fella ridin' shotgun. Just pay attention to your jobs, and don't be worryin' about who anybody is. Got it?"

"We got it," one man said, and the others nodded.

***

Clint was keeping his eye on the road for a felled tree, just in case. It was usually a sure-fire way to get a coach to stop. Or even a train, for that matter.

But he heard them even before he saw them coming at them from both sides as they rounded the bend.

"Here they come!" Clint yelled.

"Jesus," Bill said, "there's a lot of them. What do I do?"

"Make it look like we're going to try to outrun them," Clint said. "Then when I tell you to rein in, do it and grab your shotgun."

"Right!"

Clint watched the riders, saw a big man dressed in black leading one group. He decided this man was the leader, so this was the one he wanted to keep alive.

"Aren't you gonna shoot?" Bill asked.

"Not til they get closer," Clint said. "And not until they do."

"Why aren't they?"

"We'll find out," Clint said, "when they do start shooting."

Chapter Forty-Six

They started shooting, first the big, dark man, and then the others.

"You gonna shoot back now?" Bill yelled.

"Not yet."

"Why not?"

"They're not hitting anything, yet."

The approaching holdup men were firing their handguns and weren't in range to do any damage yet.

"Okay," Clint said, "I'm going to drop the lockbox, and then you rein the team in."

"You sure about this?"

"Yes!"

Clint climbed on top of the careening coach and untied the lockbox. It was very heavy, but he managed to shove it end-over-end toward the edge of the coach, and then off. It hit the ground and exploded into pieces, the contents thrown every which way.

"Now!" he yelled at Bill.

The driver yanked back on the reins several times before he managed to stop the team. The coach tilted to one side, and for a moment Clint thought they were going over, but then it righted itself and stopped.

"Let's go!" Clint yelled, jumping down.

As Highway Bill made his way down, Clint banged his hand on the coach door and said, "Now, now!"

***

The hold-up men saw the box fly from the top of the coach and come crashing down on the ground.

"The money!" one of them shouted, as the box exploded. "Get the money!"

Leo Gordon saw that Clint Adams had shoved the box off the top of the coach.

"No, no," he shouted, "keep goin'."

Half of the men stopped, turned their horses and looked at him. The others rode toward the shattered box, and its strewn contents.

"Damn it!" Gordon swore.

***

The coach door opened and Sheriff Maybe came jumping out, rifle in hand.

"There!" Clint said, pointing.

"Right!"

"The man in black," he said, "Don't kill him." Clint looked at Bill. "Got that?"

"Got it!"

The three of them began running toward the approaching men. As Clint opened fire, so did the sheriff and Highway Bill. Immediately, three men fell to the ground, and the man in black abruptly stopped. He turned to look for the rest of his men. Three were scrambling around after what had been in the lockbox. He heard a buckboard being driven off by a fourth man, which really didn't matter.

Clint told Bill, "Keep him covered," as the man in black dropped his gun. He and the sheriff kept running toward the other men.

"What the hell?" one of the men shouted. "What is this stuff?"

"It's lead," another said.

"Not gold?"

The four men stood there and stared at each other.

"Lead?" one said.

"Drop your guns!" Sheriff Maybe shouted.

The men turned in the direction of his voice.

"Don't try it," Clint said. "Just drop your guns to the ground."

"This is lead," one of them complained, "not gold."

"Who told you there'd be gold?" Clint asked.

The men dropped their guns and pointed toward the man in black.

"And what's his name?" Clint asked.

"That's Leo," one of them said, "Leo Gordon. He told us we'd all get rich."

"Then Leo Gordon is the man I want to talk to, isn't he?"

"You go ahead," Sheriff Maybe said. "I'll bring these boys along."

Clint turned and walked back to where Highway Bill was covering Leo Gordon.

"Lead?" Gordon said.

"That's right," Clint said. "Nothing but lead."

"So this was a set-up."

John C. Maybe walked the other men past Gordon and packed them into the stage.

"You're all under arrest," Clint said, "and headed back to Colorado Springs. You'll be charged with all the robberies and attempted murder."

"Now wait a minute—"

"That is," Clint said, "unless you can tell us who the ringleader of the stagecoach robberies is."

Gordon stared at Clint a moment, then said, "I think I might be able to help you with that."

Coming November 27, 2020

A Special Christmas Edition

THE GUNSMITH GIANT
THE JINGLE BELL TRAIL

Clint Adams follows the jingle bell trail to a town where
he brings Christmas cheer to a widowed mother and her
little boy.

For more information
visit: www.SpeakingVolumes.us

Coming November 2020
THE GUNSMITH GIANT
No. 1
Trouble in Tombstone

For more information
visit: www.SpeakingVolumes.us

Coming December 27, 2020
THE GUNSMITH
465
The Children of Willow Springs

For more information
visit: www.SpeakingVolumes.us

On Sale Now!

THE GUNSMITH
463
The Gunsmith Women's Club

For more information
visit: www.SpeakingVolumes.us

On Sale Now!

THE GUNSMITH *series*
Books 430 - 462

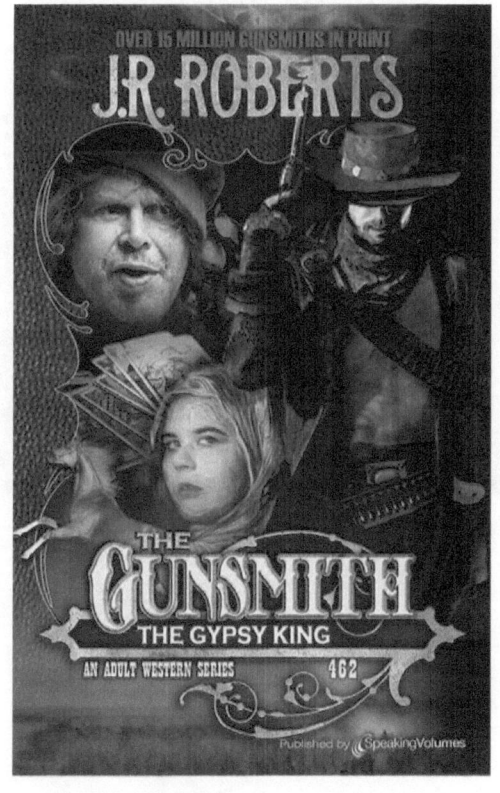

For more information
visit:

On Sale Now!

Lady Gunsmith *series*
Books 1 - 9
Roxy Doyle and the Lady Executioner

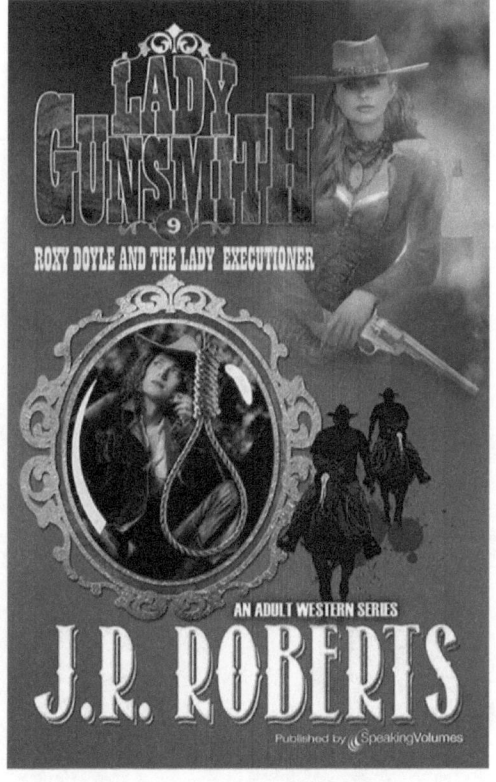

On Sale Now!

Award-Winning Author
Robert J. Randisi (J.R. Roberts)

For more information
visit:

www.ingramcontent.com/pod-product-compliance
Lightning Source LLC
Chambersburg PA
CBHW030448250626
47154CB00003BA/1175